The
Patient
in
202

A KATHY MARTIN STORY

By Josephine James

ILLUSTRATED BY
William Plummer

GOLDEN PRESS **NEW YORK**

Contents

1

Kathy Martin, Registered Nurse

It was a little after noon on Thursday, August 24th, when the four girls came out of the State Office Building in San Francisco. Kathy Martin was first through the revolving door. She was bareheaded as usual, but looked very citified in her tweed suit and gloves. She blinked at the unexpected sunlight and turned to wait for her three friends as they pushed one by one through the door.

Afterward, when the chain of events in which she was involved had become front-page news, Kathy had no difficulty remembering the day it all began. There was the date in bold, blue ink on the precious piece of paper in her hand. Dreams do come true, she thought, remembering the years of hoping, the years of studying. And now, here was the fact, right before her eyes: Katherina Nickola Elizabeth Martin, Registered Nurse!

9

"It's just a piece of paper, Martin. You needn't stare at the license as if you'd discovered a new star in the sky." Kelley Jones could never pass up a chance to tease her former roommate when "that look" came into Kathy's eyes.

Kathy laughed good-naturedly and tucked the license in its manila envelope. "O.K. So it's just words on a piece of paper. But it's a piece of paper I've been waiting for since I was eight years old, Jonesy. Now I have it, it feels strange. The end of learning, the beginning of living."

"Isn't that what we're about to go out and celebrate?" said Jenny.

Kelley and Yo and Jenny each had similar envelopes in their handbags. Now, without question, they were entitled to write R.N. after their names.

Yo Nakayama looked up at Kathy, taller than ever and much more dignified in city clothes. Yo sighed. "Getting our licenses may mean the end of studying for you and Jonesy," she said. "Me, I feel like a Probie again, except that I'm memorizing tables of atomic weights instead of *trematoda* and *streptococcus* and all the other unpronounceables at Nursing School."

The twinkle in Yo's eyes belied her sigh. She was enrolled in summer school at the University across the Bay, in Berkeley, beginning the long road to an M.D. degree. And she was blissfully happy.

Jenny Ramirez, too, was looking forward to more study when her summer job as a Visiting Nurse was over. Still,

Jenny knew what Kathy meant. Passing the State Boards was a milestone worthy of the celebration they had planned. "R.N. Day in San Francisco!"

"Do you suggest that we begin living by starving to death?" Kelley growled. "When do we eat?"

There was no need to ask where. Every detail of their holiday in the city had been planned. They intended to visit all their favorite haunts, from Sun Yat-sen's statue to the Golden Gate Bridge. For lunch Kathy had demanded a restaurant on the brow of Telegraph Hill. She'd been there only once before, with Steve Kovak, but had never stopped talking about the food and the view of the city roofs and the islands in the bay.

"On to the Castle!" she said. "We'll hoof it to Union Square and ride up Powell in Jenny's pet cable car."

"And then walk another mile to Telegraph Hill," Kelley objected. "The bus would take us right to Coit Tower." She had been working since graduation in a big hospital in San Francisco and had learned all the tricks of getting around the city.

Jenny shook her head. "Walking, we can window shop. There's Gail's wedding present to think of."

The noon sun filled the streets with a mellow light. Sidewalk flower stands combined with fresh ocean air to give out the special fragrance that belonged to San Francisco. The shops on Union Square sparkled. Clothes for the opera, clothes for the beach, a dummy clothed as a bride that looked for all the world like Gail Henderson. In the next window, bridesmaids in huge hats and flowery pink taffeta posed against a background of greenery.

Kathy groaned. "Can't you just see five-foot Yo and a beanpole like me in twin outfits?"

Gail had asked the four girls to be bridesmaids. What to wear was a problem.

"I vote for our old Probie uniforms. Striped bags are all the rage in Paris," Kelley commented cheerfully. She prided herself on caring nothing about clothes, although her exquisite sweaters and skirts were the envy of her friends. "Besides, I thought we were shopping for wedding presents—and food. I admit I need to lose ten pounds, but I don't intend to do it all this afternoon!"

A moment later, however, Kelley forgot she was hungry. They had come to a narrow shop almost hidden between imposing store fronts. No name was on the door. Except for a shimmering piece of gray brocade and a vase of chrysanthemums, there was nothing in the one small recessed window.

"Like a Cézanne still life," Kelley said admiringly. "Let's go in. I've always wanted an excuse."

"What is it?" asked Yo. "A flower shop?"

Kelley had already pushed open the door. "Of course not. You must have heard of Gray's. It's famous for art imports." Kelley had studied painting before she entered nursing school, and she expected everyone to know as much about the art world as she did.

"Proving that we're just farmers' daughters in the big city," Kathy murmured to Yo. "Apples and strawberry markets we're experts on; art shops, no."

"Unless a peach-slicing machine is a work of art, I'm with you," Jenny put in, peering over Kelley's shoulder at a thickly carpeted room, painted a soft old rose.

"Come on," Kelley urged. "We're sure to see just the right thing for Gail."

The girls found themselves alone in a room that bore no resemblance to a place of business. Teakwood chairs and a low table were grouped around a fireplace at the far end. An alabaster vase and a carved Chinese jade figure set in niches at each side of the mantel were lighted by invisible beams. A few pictures—water colors and oils—hung on the walls.

Yo and Jenny stood a bit hesitantly at the door, but Kathy tiptoed around after Kelley, her feet sinking into the thick white carpet. She stopped with delight before a painting of sand dunes and cypress trees.

"I know those trees!" she said in an awed whisper, beckoning Yo and Jenny over. "They call that bare twisted one the witch tree. Steve and I picnicked under it. Right below Carmel. See how it leans out smack over the ocean?"

"I know it, too," Yo said. "There's a whirlpool under that cliff and ships that came too close were 'bewitched' and sucked under the cliff." Yo's face brightened as she recalled the old legend, but Jenny still looked troubled.

"There's nobody here to wait on us," she said uncomfortably. "Maybe we'd better leave."

"Sh! Listen!" From somewhere in the back the sounds of a violin could be heard. "That must be Mr. Gray play-

ing." Kelley studied Kathy's picture with approval. "We
can look around. Mr. Gray's an odd character. They say
he goes up in the mountains for days, to meditate or
something. Any time the door is open, it means people
are welcome to come in and browse around."

"I still feel like a trespasser," Jenny said. "But the
music is lovely. Let's hear it to the end at least."

Kelley beamed. "The man's probably a mental case or
a genius or both. But he's made a fortune collecting
Oriental art for museums and spends it helping starving
artists."

"Like Garfield's dukes and kings in Italy that set
Michelangelo and da Vinci to painting their palace
walls?" Linda Garfield had flooded the mails with romantic postcards from all over Europe until even prac-
tical little Yo had become picture conscious this summer
—although she insisted that she'd rather have Leonardo
da Vinci's drawing of the veins and arteries in an arm
than his Mona Lisa. "I wonder if your Mr. Gray wears
doublet and hose and a gold chain around his neck,
Jonesy?"

"Only when the moon is full." A deep masculine voice
startled them. Only Jenny had noticed that the music had
stopped, and no one had seen the door in the back wall
swing open. In the doorway stood a lean, loose-jointed
man, slightly stoop-shouldered. He had a thick mop of
unruly straight hair that fell forward over keen eyes
crinkled with amusement. Craggy, rather stern features
were softened momentarily by a curiously shy smile.

Kelley was the first to recover from embarrassment. She explained with supreme confidence that they were searching for a rather special wedding present.

"Be seated, ladies," Gray gestured to the chairs. "I've taken the liberty of ordering tea—though if you'd like something different . . .?"

"All this—and nourishment, too!" Kelley murmured blissfully.

A manservant in a Roman toga rolled in a tea cart. Only after tea was drunk and an alarming number of little cakes consumed did the proprietor of the shop indicate that he had heard Kelley's request to be shown wedding gifts. He looked from one to the other of the girls and asked, "Which of you is being married?"

"Oh, it's not for us!" Kathy answered hurriedly. "The bride is a Registered Nurse. We all are—at least Gail will be as soon as she takes her State Boards. She's marrying a journalist, and we thought we could find something for all of us to give them—something beautiful. We were all in school together, and Gail directed all our plays, and . . ."

The art dealer nodded. His eyes were full of sympathy. With half a chance, Kathy would have floundered on, giving him the story of all their lives. She had never met a more perfect listener. But the man set down his tea cup and crossed the room. From a cabinet he drew a small jade bowl, sea-green shaded almost to white.

It was right as right for Gail.

Haltingly Kathy asked the price.

"Oh, I'd say about two thousand." Mr. Gray's voice seemed rather annoyed that a question of money should be raised.

Yo gasped. Her whole year at the University would cost just that!

"We'd better settle for a toaster," Jenny murmured to no one in particular.

Unabashed, Kelley rose. "We are just looking, today," she murmured.

It was a signal for escape. But on the way to the door, Kathy stopped to admire a Chinese scroll in a locked display case.

"You have good taste, my dear," Mr. Gray explained. "That's a collector's item—a rather rare 14th-century poem."

He invited them to return and gave Kelley his card. *Amos X. Gray.* Solemnly she presented the card to Kathy. "A rather rare collector's item, my dear."

The cable car was crowded with tourists. Kathy and Kelley found seats outside next to a frankly terrified old lady whose packages threatened to slip off onto the street.

The little car climbed toward the hilltop, clanging importantly as every street corner revealed wider vistas.

"There's no place like San Francisco, is there?" Kathy whispered, with a sweeping gesture toward the bay far below California Street. Her expansive gesture ended suddenly as the car hurtled down a hill even steeper than the one they had climbed.

Kelley's smile was almost motherly. "You're having fun this summer, aren't you? Are you sure you want to leave it all—your family, I mean—and Steve—to go off to Alaska?"

"Are we really going, Jonesy? Have you heard anything more? It seems kind of unreal—as if I'd dreamed the Federal Hospital in Sitka."

"It's very real, Martin. You've signed up for a year of general nursing duty—anything from dishing out drugs in Central Supply to an emergency delivery of an Eskimo baby in an igloo. We won't hear anything more from Washington until, *bingo,* our orders will come."

Kathy nodded slowly. "I know. 'Miss Jones and Miss Martin will report to the airport, Flight so-and-so, on such-and-such a day.' And we've got to be ready. State license, Red Cross Emergency course, postgraduate hospital experience . . ."

The clanging of the cable car and the conductor's warning shout, " 'Round the corner!" swallowed Kathy's next words. She fished around in her bag and pulled out a newspaper clipping. "I was planning to apply for duty at Appleton Hospital, so as to live at home this summer. But on the bus coming up this morning I saw this ad."

She handed the slip of paper to Kelley.

> **WANTED.** R.N. Vacation relief. Two weeks. Doctor's Hospital. Ocean Cliff. Immediate.

She watched Kelley read the scrap of newsprint. Ocean

Cliff was on the rugged coast between Carmel and Big Sur—Monterey pines and cypresses, rocks and ocean. Exactly like the painting in the art shop.

"What do you think?"

"A private hospital at a seaside resort?" Kelley was unenthusiastic. "Could mean just a lot of old ladies taking rest cures or fishing parties with sunburn. But it'll count for experience."

"It's a fabulous spot," Kathy said defensively.

"It is that," Kelley agreed. Hastily she gave back the slip of paper. "Come on, Martin, we have to get off at the next corner or we'll have a two-mile hike to Telegraph Hill. It's all uphill even from here." Yo and Jenny were already beckoning them to get off.

Yo and Jenny led the way through North Beach, past the pizza restaurants, the beatnik hangouts, the second-hand bookshops. Kathy and Kelley followed behind, still deep in conversation.

"Besides the coastline, there's also—well, Steve's taking this forest-fire control course. He's up and down the coast a lot. He's up this way today," she added with a casualness that was a little too casual to be convincing. "He's going to drive me home after we have dinner and watch the city lights come on from the Top of the Mark."

A shrewd glance from Kelley brought a blush to Kathy's cheeks. Her friendship with Steve Kovak had lasted through three stormy years of nursing school, and although she maintained stoutly that it was nothing more than friendship, she somehow doubted that her friends believed it. Sometimes she didn't believe it herself.

"You and Steve have been getting along well this summer, haven't you?" Kelley said.

"Wonderfully. Not more than ten fights a week."

"If Steve asked you to give up the Alaska job, would you?"

Kathy's answer was abrupt. "That's not something I have to decide. Steve wants me to go. He's all wrapped up in this forestry thing. He doesn't need me."

"And you need to be needed." Kelley nodded understandingly. That was why Kathy got such satisfaction from nursing—and why she made such a good nurse—whether for acutely ill patients or anxious old ladies with chronic ailments. "Take the relief nurse job, Martin," she advised. "After all, bedpans are bedpans, wherever they are. And a nurse never knows when she'll be called on for everything in the book."

Hours later, when Kathy was driving down the highway in Steve's little car, she was still worrying the question of job experience as a pup worries a bone.

"What do you think, Steve? Shall I try for the Ocean Cliff place? The coast is so beautiful down there. Seeing that painting of the witch tree was sort of an omen, I think, don't you?"

She had entertained Steve all through dinner with the story of their shopping in the art store and had only one small argument when Steve suggested that perhaps this Mr. Gray might be something of a phony. But now, driv-

ing home in the moonlight, Kathy's mood was serious.
She wanted Steve to say that he approved of the job at
Ocean Cliff even if she wasn't apt to have such challenging cases as Kelley had every hour in the big city hospital. She wanted him to say that he'd be coming down
the coast often, that they'd have lots of picnics under the
witch tree. Most of all she wanted Steve to say again
that he was proud of her for passing her State Boards,
that he knew she was going to make a good nurse.

They were going around the long curve to the summit
of the Santa Cruz mountains. The tall, lanky firefighter
knew every inch of the road, but in the darkness he had
to keep his mind on the driving. Kathy had to wait a
moment for her answer. When it came it was in the form
of a question.

"What did that artist guy call it? A collector's item?
Katherina Nickola Elizabeth Martin, R.N., collector's
item, rather rare. You're looking very pretty, Nurse Martin, in the light of the moon."

"Moonshine!" Kathy blushed in the darkness and tried
to think of something bright to say.

The sickening sound of skidding wheels and crashing
metal paralyzed her thoughts. As Steve's car rounded the
curve, a body hurtled to the pavement from the car
ahead.

Steve threw on his brakes and he and Kathy sprinted
forward without a word. The wheels of the wrecked car
were still spinning when they reached the spot. The
whole front end was smashed against a boulder; both

doors had flown open. Wedged between the door and embankment a foot stuck up like a signpost. The trouser leg had fallen back, revealing a stiff, white, bloodless leg. The man under the car was probably already dead.

Steve, as a fireman, was used to dealing with accidents and sudden death. A student nurse knew death as well, but neatly covered on a stretcher, or in a hospital bed.

"See to the man in the road, Kathy," Steve said quietly. "I'll take over here and radio the Ranger Station to call an ambulance." Steve returned to his car and began calling on the two-way radio.

A nurse never knows when she'll be called on for everything in the book. When Kelley had said that earlier that afternoon, Kathy hadn't thought it would come true before the day was out. She was trembling as she neared the inert figure. Suppose she couldn't remember everything? Suppose. . . .

She jerked off her gloves and knelt down in the road. It wasn't a man at all, but a boy—seventeen, eighteen—about the age of her brother Nick. Smaller than Nick though, with sandy hair, stained now with blood.

No deep cuts on the face or head, but blood was spurting from a gash on the wrist and one leg was crumpled underneath the boy. First things first. Kathy didn't have to see the bright red color to know that the rush of blood came from an artery. From a cut vein, the blood would move like a sluggish river. Quickly she ripped back the shirt sleeve. She pressed the fingers of one hand over the cut, feeling with the other hand for the pressure point in the upper arm. If the artery wasn't severed, you could stop bleeding by pressure, and a tourniquet wouldn't be necessary. You learned to try pressure first, automatically, as you learned to react automatically in every emergency.

She shook her head. Against her fingers she could feel the press of blood continuing. This one would require a tourniquet. With one hand she unknotted the scarf from around her neck. A pencil would do for a stick. There was one in her pocket. Hastily she tied the scarf around the upper arm where the faint pulse could still be felt, slipped the pencil through, and twisted the scarf tighter and tighter. Too little pressure. The arm was beginning to swell. She forced herself to make the tourniquet tighter. Even in the dim light, she could see the arm turn white. The bleeding stopped. She leaned over to the other wrist, feeling for a pulse. Very slow, very shallow and faint.

"Can you hear me?" she said, putting her lips close to the gray-white face. Eyelids flickered and lips moved slightly, but no sound came.

"He's just a boy, Steve," she called. "Alive, but in shock. His leg seems to be broken. High, near the hip. Bring me your coat, will you? The only thing we can do is to keep him warm."

The boy's hands were clammy and cold. The left hand gripped a torn bit of paper.

Kathy rubbed the boy's fingers. Circulation returned ever so slightly. The scrap of paper dropped beside her.

Steve had come up with a flashlight and Kathy tried to see if there was anything written on the paper. A name, perhaps, or some clue of identification. No, the paper was blank.

There had been no other cars on the road, but suddenly five or six materialized. A highway patrolman arrived and then, sirens wide open, an ambulance.

"Plasma needed here," Kathy said to the ambulance attendant. "The boy's in shock. I'm an R.N. I'll help you administer it."

Taking the boy's pulse for the second time, Kathy could hear Steve and the patrolman talking. The policeman was taking down the name and license number of the owner from the license taped to the bent steering wheel.

"Maxfield! Ed Maxfield from Carmel . . . Why, I gave him a ticket for speeding only last week! Not the first one either. He's one of those wise guys who believe they don't have to obey the law because they've been driving for thirty years. Now look at 'im, getting plasma in the dirt of the road."

"But he's just a boy, officer," Steve said.

"You're right," the patrolman said, stepping closer. "I see now it isn't Maxfield, but what—"

Steve pointed to the figure on the other side of the car, and Kathy could hear the policeman's shocked exclamation. Death wasn't something you got used to, even if you were a highway patrolman.

The ambulance driver came up. "Hold the apparatus

steady, lady, while we lift the boy to the stretcher. We'll let the plasma drip while we make the run to the hospital."

"That tourniquet has to be watched. Do you want me to go along?" Kathy asked after the patient was safely in the ambulance.

A nurse was pledged to devote herself to the welfare of those committed to her care. That was part of the Florence Nightingale Oath.

"We'll manage," the driver answered.

"I'm a nurse," Kathy insisted. "An R.N."

"She's got the papers with her to prove it," Steve interjected in an amused voice. "Right in our car."

He had left the patrolman radioing for a second ambulance to take the body of Edwin Maxfield to the morgue. Kathy looked a little edgy, and the best cure for nerves, in Steve's opinion, was a little teasing.

The ambulance driver winked. "Just finished your State Boards, I bet. I've got a sister felt the same way when she got that piece of paper in her hands." Then he added in a more serious voice, "All the same, you did a good job. I wish every accident victim we picked up had such expert care."

II

Four-Legged Fielder

Time, at the Martin ranch, was measured off not in ordinary weeks and months, but in the blossoming, the ripening, the harvesting of the apples. Kathy's Yugoslav grandfather had been one of the immigrants who introduced apple growing into the valley. The first trees he planted had long since ceased bearing, to be replaced one by one by young saplings. These in turn had grown old and wide-spreading until they covered most of the upland in gently curving rows.

Gravensteins, Newtons, Pippins and a few of the small, tart, red Winesaps ripened in succession from the end of August to Halloween. Picking time had begun for the green-skinned Gravensteins. Late in the morning after the San Francisco jaunt, Kathy was out on the knoll where Gravensteins grew, helping her father and her

brother Nick harvest the crop. Tall and slim in blue
jeans and a work shirt, she had tied her hair back in a
bright red bandana.

As a rule, she and her eighteen-year-old brother made
a gay thing of the picking and tossed lively chatter back
and forth. Today Kathy picked in silence. She had slept
badly. All night she had been disturbed by dreams of
the broken bodies on the Santa Cruz highway. But now,
out of doors, the accident was fading from her mind. She
loved to work with her father among the apple trees. Big
Nick, as everyone called him, belonged to the land as
surely as the tree trunks and the tawny turf. Little Nick
—now as tall as his father—moved with a quicker rhythm.
He was trying to crowd in more work than a man could
do. He was leaving for the Agricultural School at Davis
as soon as the university opened. With Kathy going to
Alaska as soon as her orders came, that would leave only
eight-year-old Johnny to help out at home. Johnny—and
Spot, the black and white cocker.

Kathy had filled her third bushel basket and started
for another empty when she saw Johnny and the dog
trudging up the path from the back door.

"Johnny's already put on his Little League uniform,"
Kathy laughed. "I must say I can't give an orchid to who-
ever picked it out. That suit is big enough for three of
Johnny."

"He always gets dressed hours before a game. He did
it even when he was just a bench-warmer." Nick grinned.
"He'd sleep in the thing if Mama would let him."

For months, Johnny had talked nothing but baseball. In July he'd been taken to San Francisco to see the Giants and had collected three autographs on his baseball cards, which he counted and sorted interminably.

"At last count," Nick said, "it was five hundred and seventy-four—but he thought he might have missed a few, so he'll count again tomorrow. Mom shudders every time she picks one up off the floor. He even plows through the papers for batting averages."

As Johnny made his way up the path, he waved a newspaper and shouted something they couldn't understand.

"The Giants' latest triumph, no doubt," Nick muttered. "Was I ever that nuts about baseball?"

"Appleton didn't have Little League when you were growing up. But I seem to remember a few months back, when you were playing football . . ."

"What is Johnny saying, Kathy?" Big Nick's voice boomed out from the thick tree branches. Only his long legs were visible on the stepladder; his shoulders and head were high in the treetop. "What's this about your picture in the paper?"

The big man did not wait for an answer. He climbed down the ladder and reached for the paper in Johnny's hand. A pudgy finger pointed to a picture opposite the sports page. "Monterey Artist Meets With Fatal Accident," was the caption.

"There, Papa. I was reading about the Giants, and I saw Kathy's picture. It looked like Kathy, and I read what was under the picture and it's got Kathy's name. *Miss Katherina Martin.* I read it by myself."

Mr. Martin held the paper at arm's length and squinted. He had recently been advised to wear eyeglasses, but they were never at hand when he wanted them. Laboriously he read aloud:

Edwin Maxfield was dead on arrival at Santa Cruz Hospital, and Collin Monroe, driver of the car, was seriously injured when the car in which they were riding crashed into a boulder on Route 1 at 10:45 p.m. last night. First on the scene of the accident were Stephen S. Kovak of the County Forest Fire Prevention Service, and Miss Katherina Martin, R.N., of Appleton. Miss Martin administered first aid.

"You didn't say a word about that," young Nick said, looking at his sister curiously.

"I didn't do very much. Stopped a cut from bleeding and then did nothing till the ambulance came. The boy was in shock. There wasn't anything much to do. The dead man . . ." She shivered a little, remembering the bloodless leg sticking up against the cliff. "He was pinned under the car, between the car and the boulder. What did the paper say the boy's name was, Papa? Collins?"

"Collin Monroe. Here, take the paper. I'm going back to my apples." Big Nick was disappointed. He had expected something pleasant about Kathy, perhaps the news about her getting her certificate in nursing.

"Collin Monroe. It's a pleasant name, isn't it? He's about your age, Nick, but about a foot shorter. I think he's got a fractured hip. It wasn't any fun seeing a body come flying through the air. I'd just as soon forget it."

"Well, I thought you'd like to see your name in the paper. I found it myself," Johnny said, a bit crestfallen.

"You're a fine reader, Johnny," Kathy said.

She smiled down at her small brother. Kathy had rather regretfully outgrown dolls when Johnny was born, and she had been a second mother to him. Caring for Johnny through measles and mumps and chicken pox had been her first real nursing experience. In Johnny's eyes, Kathy was nothing less than perfect. She didn't intend to let him down now by not showing interest in his reading prowess.

"I read the baseball news every day," he said, brightening. "Oh, there was something else. Mom said come in right away and eat, so she can get the dishes washed before we go to the game. You know I'm the regular left fielder now, Kathy. Today is a real, real important game. We're tied for first place."

Appleton had no professional baseball team. The newly organized Little League that summer was the center of interest, and not only for the Martin household. When their pickup truck pulled into the high school parking lot, the bleachers were half full.

"You hold Spot. And remember, we're the home team. Watch for me." Johnny thrust the dog into Kathy's arms and disappeared importantly toward the improvised dugout.

Young Nick grinned. "That's what you get for being a softy. 'Spot ought to see a ball game,' Johnny says! After I put that pooch out of the truck!"

"Well, after all, he chases balls for Johnny every morning," Mrs. Martin said.

"You'll have to admit he looks expectant—just like all the fathers. The mothers just look anxious," Kathy whispered. "Look at that redhead in slacks. She'll have a heart attack if she doesn't calm down."

"That's Ronny's mother," Mrs. Martin said. "Ronny pitches. So much depends on good pitching, naturally she's worried. Not many balls come Johnny's way in left field. But I die a thousand deaths every time he comes to bat."

"Three months ago, Mom thought a bat was a barn pest," Nick teased. "Now she's an expert."

"It is as important to Johnny, Nicholas, as football was to you." Big Nick's tone was a bit severe. "For an eight-year-old, Johnny does very well at the bat. I think you should be proud of him." Clearly, Johnny's father was proud of his youngest.

Conversation ceased when the umpires walked onto the field. Even Spot sat up straight and pricked up his ears.

"Who's the man behind the plate, Papa?" Kathy asked.

"George O'Malley. You remember him, don't you, from the apple shed?" Her father was leaning forward, his knees almost touching the back of the man ahead. "A nice man, but when he doesn't get enough sleep, sometimes he makes bad mistakes about the strikes and balls."

"Little League umpires are brave men." Ella Martin laughed. "George doesn't know the danger he's in when he calls a third strike on our Johnny!"

Kathy wasn't much of a baseball fan, but she found herself interested as the game went on. "The kids play as if their lives depended on it," she commented to her mother.

"That's true, Kathy," Ella Martin replied. "Sometimes I wonder if the competition isn't too strongly built up." Then, as Johnny came up to bat, she forgot the competition and shouted, "Come on, Johnny, get a hit!" right along with Big Nick.

Johnny did get a hit, and scored a run. His team was leading by three runs until the top of the fifth inning. There were two outs. The bases were loaded. A ball was hit over Johnny's head. It came rolling toward the bleachers where the Martins were sitting. Johnny raced across the field after the ball. Then disaster struck. Before he could scoop it up for the throw to third base, Spot wriggled out of Kathy's arms and was flying across the field. There was a ball, and there was Johnny—to the little cocker that meant a ball game! With the greatest of ease, his four legs outran Johnny's two. Triumphantly he seized the ball and danced around his young master. From the field, Kathy could hear Johnny's agonized shriek.

"Spot, drop it. Drop that ball."

Spot was too excited to obey. He caught sight of the runner rounding second base. Away he went with Johnny chasing hot on his heels. The second baseman, the shortstop and the pitcher joined Johnny in the chase. At third base, Spot crashed into the speeding runner. The runner tripped—and Spot dropped the ball.

"Fetch, Spot, fetch!" Johnny gasped.

Spot decided to obey—in due time. Joyfully he picked up the ball, threw it a little ahead of him, captured it again, and brought it, at last, to Johnny, barking for more of this unexpected play.

All four runs scored before Johnny could get the ball back to the plate. The stands were in an uproar of laughter and groans and applause as each run scored. The plate umpire called time out as the manager of Johnny's team rushed on to the field, hollering "Interference!" A hasty conference was called and the decision was: Since the dog belonged to the fielder, interference could not be called. The runs would count!

"Those umpires don't know any more baseball than Spot," young Nick growled.

"It just isn't fair," Kathy wailed, clutching Spot with an iron grip.

The umpire wasn't forgiven until the end of the sixth (and last) inning, when in a burst of glory Johnny hit a grand slam home run and his team went ahead to win the game by a score of 12-11.

"What a game!" exclaimed Big Nick, as he steered the pickup out of the lot. "Ten hours of harvesting and loading our apples leaves me less tired than your Little League games, Johnny."

Kathy sank back into the seat beside her father. "And I thought a leisurely afternoon at the ball park would be a good time to talk about that job at Ocean Cliff," she sighed.

III

Surprise at Ocean Cliff

"Looks more like a country club than a hospital," Steve said when he drove Kathy down the coast for an interview with the director of Ocean Cliff Hospital.

Modern wings, outstretched from the center, gave the building the look of a giant sea gull hovering over a high cliff. Even in the morning fog, the construction of glass brick and aluminum and concrete was brilliantly white against the deep gray of the Pacific. Masses of zinnias and low-growing junipers outlined the driveway. A fountain, light as ocean spray, played in the center of the lawn, and the wind-blown cypresses Kathy loved made a pattern of light and shade against the sky. But she was too nervous to enjoy the beauty.

She fingered the bedraggled clipping and her knees quaked as she edged out of the car.

"I won't keep you waiting long. They'll probably throw me out anyhow. 'Of course, Miss Martin, you are an experienced nurse?' 'Well—uh—uh my license is r-rather new, Mrs. Whosis-whatsis.' 'Well, really, my dear . . . you get some experience and then come back. Goodbye.' How does anybody ever get a first job, anyhow, Steve? Or live through the interview?"

Steve smiled his slow, wide smile. "Are you going for a screen test, Miss Martin?" he said.

Kathy laughed in spite of herself, remembering the day on the bus three years ago when she'd gone for her interview with Miss Wilson at San Tomás Nursing School. That had been just after the fire at Appleton High School when she had met Steve. He had asked the same question on the bus as he sat down beside her, in the same deep voice that combined admiration with an irresistible urge to tease.

"Remember how I burst forth with a corny speech on service to humanity and following the footsteps of Florence Nightingale? What a headful of romantic notions I had about nursing!"

"And you're no longer interested in service to humanity and following in the footsteps?"

"Oh, Steve, of course I am. But you know what I mean—" Kathy suddenly became aware of Steve's twinkling eyes. "Steve Kovak, if you don't stop teasing me!"

"All right, beautiful. But don't look so doleful. Just prance up to that big glass door as if you're doing the hospital a favor—as you are." Steve leaned over and

patted Kathy lightly on the shoulder. "They're getting
the best relief nurse this side of the moon. Now go in
there and knock 'em dead!"

Fifteen minutes later Kathy came swinging confidently
across the parking lot and settled down in the car before
Steve could untangle his long legs to open the door for
her. She pulled off the hat she had bought for the interview, tossed it to the back and let the sea breeze blow
through her short brown curls.

"Relief nurse! It's a good name. I'm relieved that's
over!"

Steve grinned. "I gather you got the job?"

Kathy nodded. "Martin luck. Their regular staff nurse
is marrying a soldier during her two weeks off. They had
to have somebody right away. The nursing director is the
executive type. Likes to have plenty of nurses to stand
between her and the patients. Efficient nurses, of course.
She raised an eyebrow at the date on my license. Then
she saw my San Tomás diploma. And, Steve, she knows
Miss Wilson! Old Ironsides did the trick," Kathy went on
gleefully, using Miss Wilson's nickname among San
Tomás nursing students. "I gave her my letter of recom-
mendation—the one Miss Wilson gave me before I grad-
uated—and she gobbled it up with one efficient glance
and said, 'Very well, Miss Martin. Miss Wilson does not
lightly recommend inexperienced girls.' I report for duty
tomorrow afternoon. I'll work the three to eleven shift.
And I'll live in that cute little cottage we passed—the one
out on the rocks. Let's go on down to Carmel, Steve, and

picnic under the witch tree." She reached over to the back seat, where the picnic hamper was. "In fact, I think I'll fortify myself with a ham sandwich on the way. I'm starved. I was too scared to eat breakfast. Have one?"

Next day Kathy came down from Appleton alone on the bus. She stopped off at the nurses' cottage to leave her suitcase and change into her uniform. The housekeeper showed her to a plain, low-ceilinged room. Two beds, a bureau and a desk filled almost every foot of space, but the view through the window was all ocean —a brilliant deep blue today, sparkling with whitecaps. And it was quiet—so quiet that through the open window Kathy could hear the whirring wings of cormorants swirling around an island beyond the steep cliff.

"Miss Gregory is the name of your roommate," the housekeeper said. "She won't worry you any. She's gone by six-thirty in the morning for day duty. You're on PM shift, right?"

Kathy nodded.

"You won't hardly see each other," the housekeeper went on. "You know how it is."

Kathy knew. At the nursing residence at San Tomás there was always somebody sleeping, somebody else getting ready to go on duty. Roommates on different shifts were rarely together. Still, when they did meet, there were thousands of things to talk about.

Pinning on her cap before the mirror, Kathy was suddenly homesick for school. Here there would be no

Kelley, no Gail to gossip with. No Linda to look after. No Miss Wilson, no Mrs. Seaforth to tide her over moments of doubt and anxiety.

You're twenty-one years old, Kathy Martin. She made a face at the frightened-looking girl in the mirror. *You can't go to school forever. You wanted the job. Now you've got it. So stop fiddling with your cap and march up that hill to work. And look calm and cheerful, as if you knew what you were doing.* Obediently the image in the mirror put on a "walking-into-a-patient's-room" expression. At least Kathy hoped it was. She felt like a patient herself as she squared her shoulders and set forth across the lawn.

"Miss Martin? You're expected," a young girl at the front desk said. "The nurse's station is down the corridor to the right. That's the med-surg wing. The other is maternity. You have a few minutes, don't you? I could show you around the offices and kitchen and Central Supply. They're all in this central section behind me."

The girl chattered along as she pointed out the business offices, the records room. "I want to work in Records next summer, if my shorthand is good enough. I think Records is so educational, don't you? You won't have any trouble finding your way around here. I guess coming from a city hospital like San Tomás, our hospital looks kind of small. You are from San Tomás, aren't you? Because of your cap with the black stripe? I collect nurses' caps the way some of the kids at school collect foreign cars—trying to see how many different ones they can tell

apart, I mean. Nurses' caps are more fun," she added
with a shy smile. "I think nursing is wonderful."

"Do you want to be a nurse?"

"How did you guess?" The girl grinned broadly. "I'm
still in high school, just working here summers. But I
want to study nursing more than anything in the world."

Kathy forgot she was lonely, forgot this was her first
real job. "That's how I was," she said warmly. "And
nursing is super." She glanced at her watch. "Time to go
over patients' charts. You keep on wanting," she said to
the eager girl. "I'll be seeing you."

The head nurse wore the wide-winged cap of the San
Francisco School of Nursing. She was of medium height,
middle-aged, neither homely nor handsome. Even her
name—Mrs. Smith—was medium! She gave Kathy a businesslike greeting and motioned to a chair. "Sorry I can't
show you around the hospital, but I'm alone. Gregory,
the day nurse, left a few minutes early. She was on her
way to Pebble Beach."

"The girl at the front desk showed me the layout, Mrs.
Smith. It seems very complete. And it's wonderful, isn't
it, for every patient to see such a beautiful view from
his window?"

"Sally takes a rather romantic view of hospital life,
Miss Martin." The head nurse looked down at her paper-
filled desk. "She's from the country—and very young."

"Sally wants to be a nurse—"

"I know," Mrs. Smith said drily. "Suppose we go over
your charts. You'll find our patients different from those

in a city hospital. Not so many acute cases, more chronic patients in private rooms."

Rich old ladies taking rest cures! Kelley had predicted it. Not very good experience for Alaska. Kathy's spirits sank.

"You have eight rooms, fourteen beds," Mrs. Smith continued. "One R.N. and two aides on duty to a shift. Except myself, of course, and the private-duty nurses. The rooms are numbered in the hundreds on the garden side, in the two-hundreds on the ocean side." Mrs. Smith picked up a chart. "101 has a private nurse on PM. Diabetes case. Female, aged 59. You'll have no duties there. Two beds in 102. Pneumonia convalescent in Bed A. Male. Oxygen tent until yesterday. Medication as indicated. Extra nourishments. Routine convalescent care. Bed B. Chronic. Cerebral accident—stroke, that is— paralyzed on left side. Needs frequent turning and he's heavy, so get your aide to help you. Restless, irritable, speech almost impossible to understand."

I'd be irritable too, if I'd been here that long, Kathy thought, glancing at the chart two inches thick.

Mrs. Smith leafed hurriedly through the charts. "Young woman in 104. In for tests. Tentative diagnosis, pernicious anemia. Keeps her light on more than necessary."

"She's frightened?" Kathy asked.

"Maybe. But she could do a lot more for herself. Wants to be babied." Rapidly the older nurse ran down the list of remaining cases—so rapidly that Kathy felt thoroughly confused.

"I can study the charts when I make out my jot sheet," she said to herself, when suddenly her attention was held. "The patient in 202—male—accident case—fractured hip. Severe contusions, chest and head. Mild concussion. Lacerations, no infection. One deep one in the left wrist, however, that isn't healing as fast as it might. No visitors other than his parents. He's a local boy, moved down from Santa Cruz this morning. Rather a foolhardy move, in my opinion, but the parents wanted him nearby. They run a gift shop and fishing place on the wharf in Monterey. Seems the boy was driving someone else's car. The owner—a very fine artist—was killed. However—"

"Is—is his name Collin Monroe? Sandy-haired? Looks about eighteen?" Kathy stammered. Not once had Mrs. Smith mentioned a name. The sick people in her apparently efficient care were cases, not people.

"Monroe is the name. I hadn't noticed the color of his hair," Mrs. Smith answered. "Is he a friend of yours, Martin? That might make it awkward. I was about to say that the patient is not to know about Edwin Maxfield's death or to talk about the accident. Doctor's orders; you'll find a note on the chart. Seems the boy was in shock and bleeding arterially from that left wrist. A nurse in a passing car applied a tourniquet, saw that he got plasma promptly. I hear she's going to get a written citation from the Highway Patrol for saving his life."

Kathy blushed to the roots of her hair. "I—I hadn't heard about the citation, Mrs. Smith. I really didn't do anything unusual. Standard first aid treatment—stopped bleeding, kept him warm and held the jar while an ambulance attendant administered plasma."

The older woman looked up in surprise. "You were the nurse? Then you'll understand the doctor's concern." A twinkle came into her eye that made her look almost human. "Our Sally will get a thrill," she murmured. "To have a celebrity as our relief nurse . . ."

IV

Collin

"Hi, Collin! Dig this fudge sludge!"

Kathy stood in the door of Room 202, balancing a double chocolate malted on the tray of afternoon nourishments. Ten days of nursing at Ocean Cliff had already gone by. She moved like an old hand through the PM routine. Midafternoon nourishments, medication as indicated on her jot sheet, TPR charting—the measuring and recording of temperature, pulse and respiration for each patient. A quick coffee break on the patio within sound and sight of the surf. Back on the floor to help the aides with the supper trays; feeding a paralyzed patient, coaxing another to feed himself. A turn at the nurse's station while Mrs. Smith had her dinner. If her charts were up to date and no doctors came she could snatch time at the desk for a note to Kelley or Gail about the

wedding plans. Then there came a strenuous hour of
back rubs and bedtime care. She had her own supper
down in the staff dining room and then went back upstairs to work through the long evening hours—the restless time for patients.

It was in those hours of darkness that Collin Monroe
asked for Edwin Maxfield and wanted to talk about the
accident. Though the fractured hip was healing, he was
uncomfortable in the long body cast and had trouble
sleeping. His mind worked overtime—and so did the
signal light clipped to his pillow. From the first night
Kathy had responded to Collin's signals as promptly as
she could. Patiently she raised or lowered the bed, and
turned the dial on his transistor radio to get the bass
player or the "far-out" horn he wanted. Patiently she let
him talk about the Monterey Jazz Festival he was missing or the "cool cats" at the North Beach night club he'd
been to with Mr. Maxfield. They had gone there the
night of the accident. It was when the inevitable questions came about the smashed car or about the "No Visitors" sign on the door that Kathy searched frantically
for ways to divert the boy's train of thought. *Doctor's
orders. Keep patient from dwelling on the accident. Must
not learn of Maxfield's death.*

Collin had never asked directly about Maxfield; had
never, in fact, mentioned his name except when he talked
about the night club. Yet it was obvious that questions
were pressing on his mind, questions that he didn't want
to ask but couldn't forget.

A nurse must learn to "read" her patient and get through to him at his own level. Kathy knew a little jive talk from her own high school days—from Don Ames, whose brother played in a combo; from the glamorous Lucille, who had gone to Hollywood to become a model; from Tony Ellsworth, now with the marines in Japan. She was no expert, but she sensed somehow that the language of jazz, of the beatnik era was something that tried to reach across barriers of communication. So, for Collin, she had set aside the dignified language becoming a newly licensed R.N.

"What's got you bugged?" she asked lightly, during a particularly trying evening, when Collin's light had flashed on continually. The diversion worked wonders. The troubled look disappeared, for the moment, from Collin's eyes and he looked beyond Kathy's stiff-starched uniform and cap to see a girl not too much older than himself.

"You're real hip! My folks don't dig that kind of talk. They say it's O.K. to be an artist, but they want me to talk like a shoe salesman. They can't understand that somebody has to fracture the language every few years to keep it alive. Like the doctor can't understand I have to see Max—I need to talk to Maxfield . . ."

"I'm not really hip to the new jive talk," Kathy put in hurriedly. "You'll have to be my teacher."

"Better not so hip than super-hip," Collin said solemnly. "The super-hips, they're all talking cats, nothing real to them. The artists—the ones who are really real, you know, they make up the language as it comes. It's just, like, a way of saying nothing by making with a lot of words . . . or saying everything by talking a lot of nothing. Couple of cats need to get through to each other, they find some cool, clean talk that isn't, like, all used up. Dig me?"

"I dig," Kathy had lied cheerfully. "Now let me, like, cool down those pillows and turn out the light. You need to sleep."

In the next few days, through the new line of communication, Collin had revealed at least a portion of his restless mind to Kathy. He loved jazz. It had taken him years to decide whether he'd rather make pictures or music, and he still rested from his art work by playing the drums.

Every day when she came on duty Collin had greeted Kathy with all the warmth of a co-conspirator and a string of new expressions that would have surprised a dyed-in-the-wool cool cat. Only the night before, Kathy had come into the room to find him laughing aloud. "Listen!" he'd commanded, and proceeded to give a creditable drum performance by tapping his cast with his knuckles, a glass straw and a pencil. "Just call me the master blaster on the plaster," Collin had said triumphantly as Kathy left for the night.

But today Collin failed to respond to Kathy's newest invention. She crossed to his bedside. The boy didn't speak. He just stared at the ceiling. His eyes were too bright, his cheeks flushed.

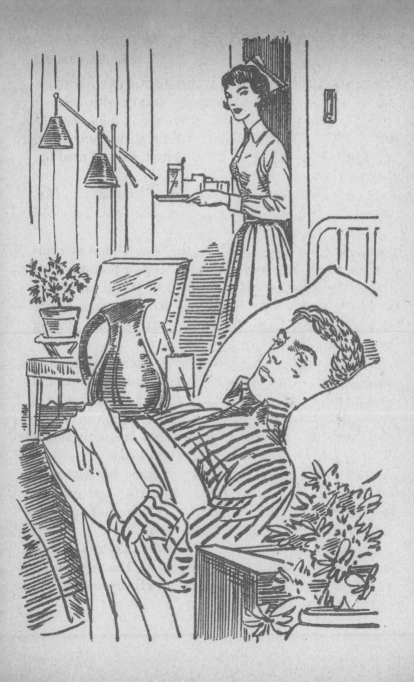

Kathy set the tall glass down without pressing him to sip it. Hurriedly she finished distributing fruit juice or milkshakes or tea to the other patients, along with afternoon medications. This duty she could not delegate to an aide. Medication was given only by an R.N.

Then she returned to Room 202 to take Collin's temperature and pulse. As she suspected, he was feverish. His pulse was fast and irregular.

Had she overlooked any notation on the chart? Gregory, the day nurse and Kathy's roommate, had not mentioned any new symptoms, and the doctor, who had seen Collin around noon, had given no new orders.

She needed time to think. She moved quietly around the room, rearranging the row of carved animals on the dresser, admiring a new one. Collin's mother must have brought it when she came to visit him that morning.

Kathy had never met the parents. Their visits were sandwiched between the early morning fishing trips and the opening of the gift shop. But Collin's room was filled with evidences of their affection for the boy—flowers, artistic knickknacks, books, papers, magazines.

The sun was very bright over the water. Kathy adjusted the curtain. The sea was glassy still, the shallow water at the shore green with seaweed. Farther out, it was pure blue, shading to violet on the horizon.

"There's a sailboat, Collin. I'm going to move your bed a little so you can see it. A real cool craft."

Like most boys, Collin was interested in every kind of ship on the coast, but he did not glance out of the window. As she moved the bed, Kathy noticed a scrap of newspaper that had slipped down between the bed and the wall. "Missed by the cleaning woman," she said to herself. She started to drop it in the wastebasket, and then, on an impulse, folded it and quietly slipped it in the pocket of her uniform.

"Is the cast bothering you, Collin? Would you like something for pain?"

Collin shrugged. "I don't need anything. Just let me alone, will you?"

The boy's voice was strained almost to breaking, and so low that Kathy had to bend down to catch the words.

A string of possibilities were running through her mind. Infection from the cut. Some kind of trouble from the severe chest bruises. A complication involving the hip fracture. *Wait a minute, Martin,* she said to herself. *You've got a license as a nurse, not as a doctor.*

"You flash your light if you want anything," she said and left the room swiftly. Down at the nurse's station, she called Dr. McLean at his unlisted home number and reported on the patient—elevated temperature, fast, irregular pulse, flushed face, respirations slow and shallow, sudden listlessness, no complaint of pain.

On the doctor's instructions she called the lab technician. Infection might have set in even though there was no localized pain. A white blood count would have to be taken.

By the time the lab technician had come and gone, there was a rush of work at the hospital. A new patient in 103, an emergency appendectomy. There was only one surgical nurse on duty and Kathy had to leave the floor to act as circulating or "dirty" nurse in surgery—to carry away unsterile instruments, gauze squares and in general, keep the operating room in order. In a small hospital, you pitched in wherever you were needed.

Mrs. Smith looked after Collin, and when Kathy returned to the floor he had fallen asleep. The lab report had come back with a negative report—no sign of the increased white blood count that would be evidence of infection. By the end of her shift, Kathy was thoroughly worn out. Her roommate, Nadine Gregory, was half asleep with the light still on. Kathy was undressing for bed when the folded piece of newspaper fell out of her pocket. She picked it up from the floor and glanced at it.

The torn sheet was from a San Francisco paper, the one Matt had gone to work for. She spread the crumpled sheet out and began reading idly.

"Greg!" The alarm in her voice made her roommate sit bolt upright in bed. "Listen!" Kathy went on. "Collin knows . . . Look at this. In the arts section. 'Memorial Exhibit for the late Edwin Maxfield. Marine paintings by Edwin Maxfield, who was fatally injured in an automobile accident last month, will be on exhibition at the Center Gallery beginning next Monday.' That's what's wrong with the boy."

Nadine was too sleepy to be interested. "What a time of night to be playing who-done-it with your patients' woes! I guess 202 is getting along all right."

"You mean he *was* getting along all right." Kathy explained the new problem. "Greg, I think you should take this clipping to Mrs. Smith tomorrow."

"I'll mention it to her, though I don't know what she can do about it. What a rough way for the boy to get the news, though. Something like this was bound to happen. I wanted to tell him right away—this business of hush-hush with patients always seems to boomerang." She lay down and pulled the covers around her shoulders. "Don't look so stricken, Martin. They'll give him a sedative and he'll sleep it off. In a day or two he will have accepted Maxfield's death as one of the facts of life."

"But it's worse for him than just losing a friend," Kathy argued. "Maxfield was his teacher and Collin's been living at the Maxfield ranch all summer, as a kind of apprentice. And he was driving the car. He's an artist, you know —with an artist's temperament, sensitive, high-strung and all that. He undoubtedly feels responsible for the man's death. What do you think we ought to do?"

"Do? Follow his doctor's orders, of course. We're nurses, remember? Not M.D.'s. Collin Monroe will be O.K. by morning."

Kathy hung her uniform on a hanger. "I hope so, Greg. He looked so wretched, staring at the ceiling, with his body all frozen in that cast. Didn't say a word to me except 'let me alone.' And he wouldn't even let me give him a backrub."

"Martin." Greg raised up on one elbow. "I'm going to give you some advice. After all, I've been nursing now for five years, day in and day out. Sure, we're 'dedicated to the alleviation of human suffering,' like it says in the textbooks. But your hours of duty are 3 to 11 p.m. It's now after midnight. You have to forget the patients at the Ocean Cliff Hospital or you'll go nuts. Put your mind on that good-looking beau of yours. Didn't you say he was going to come down this way tomorrow morning?"

Kathy nodded, her face brightening a little. "We're supposed to go on a picnic in a dreamy cove we found last week. It's right at the mouth of a little creek where the water goes in both directions—tide coming in and river flowing out—and you can stand on a rock and count five waterfalls on the cliff above. Turn around and there's the Pacific behind you. But Steve's not exactly my beau. At least, I'm not in love with him. I don't *think* I am."

Nadine chuckled as she turned out her light. "You're not? Then why do you keep that fireman's badge he gave you pinned under your pillow?"

Kathy was glad the light was out. "Anyhow," she said, "Steve will think of something I can do for Collin. He was driving when we saw the accident, you know. But I haven't much more time to do anything for anybody. Do you realize my two weeks at Ocean Cliff are almost up?"

V

On the Way to Silver Spoon

Kathy's last days at Ocean Cliff were clouded by the feeling that she was leaving a job undone. The thought of Collin Monroe continued to disturb her during three frantic days at home preparing to leave for Gail's wedding. On the morning of the fourth day, the whole family drove her to San Tomás to get the bus for the Hendersons' home in Nevada.

"Silver Spoon Junction! Is it really a place? I'll believe it when I see it, not before." Jenny Ramirez sank into the seat beside Kathy just as the bus rolled away from the San Tomás depot.

"The ticket agent sold my ticket without batting an eye," Kathy said, as she swung Jenny's bag up beside her own.

"Mine, too," Jenny admitted. "I dashed up at the last

minute and he murmured something about the Junction getting quite a crowd today."

Kathy laughed. "The family brought me up from Appleton and Johnny talked so loud about the wedding that a little old lady waiting to buy a ticket thought I was the bride and fluttered around us like an excited butterfly. I hope you don't mind taking the bus. Steve said to tell you he was sorry not to drive us. There's a fire over in the Cromwell State Forest that he had to check on. Some possibility it might go out of control."

"Will he miss the wedding?"

"Perish the thought! Steve won't let Matt down even if he has to drive all night—unless the fire gets really out of hand. But Mom didn't think we ought to take the chance of waiting for him. Gail seemed so anxious for us to come early. And part of the fun of being a bridesmaid is helping to get things ready and opening presents and trying on dresses."

Kathy had barely finished her dress in time. Kelley had chosen the material—a beautiful raw silk from Chinatown—and had sketched the design. Chrysanthemums massed at the flower stands on Union Square had been her inspiration, she wrote. She had chosen shades of yellow, from a tawny gold for Kathy's brown hair to the greenish beige of unripe apricots to set off Yo's black hair and olive skin.

"What color is your dress?" Kathy asked.

"Buttercup yellow. I never had anything so pretty. Grandmother lent me her mantilla to wear if it gets cold at the reception." Jenny chuckled and smoothed the sleeve of her red wool suit. "I borrowed this from my cousin. And the necklace is Mama's," she said, frankly amused. "The Ramirez clan sent me off in style. It's my first real vacation since I went to Girl Scout Camp when I was fourteen."

Jenny's life was different from the rest of the girls'. She had worked her way through high school and nursing school cutting fruit at the canneries in the summer, at night and on weekends; and from the day of graduation had worked as a Visiting Nurse. But being a Visiting Nurse was what Jenny wanted above everything. Even though she had won her scholarship to go back to State College for courses in Public Health Nursing, she planned to keep her job while she continued schooling.

"How is the work going?" Kathy asked.

"Good," Jenny answered. She looked out of the window a moment in silence, though there was nothing to see. The bus was lurching through a canyon, and they were walled in on both sides by brown, September-dry cliffs. "It's good," she repeated. "But harder than I thought it would be because there's so much that needs doing and so little you can do. Every day I get called to homes where people have waited too long to call a doctor because they couldn't pay. Or haven't given their kids the medication the doctor prescribed because it's so expensive. And money's not the whole trouble. One day last week, Martin, I decided I didn't want to be a nurse. It seemed too hard."

Not want to be a nurse? *Jenny Ramirez?* Kathy was startled to see tears in Jenny's eyes.

"It was a throat cancer case. A young man—about our age. Operated on at County, and home in his one room to convalesce. I'd been going by every day or two to change the dressing."

"He didn't die, did he?" Kathy asked. Losing a patient was something you didn't get accustomed to.

Jenny shook her head. "He's recovering nicely. Of course, you can't tell about cancer—not for about five years. He can't speak yet, though, and when he does, you know how his voice will sound, without a larynx."

"But he has to expect that, Jenny—and people manage."

"Mario doesn't expect it. And he won't manage—ever. He's a singer, Kathy. His buddy came yesterday while I was there. Brought his guitar—and a singing contract for Mario. Ten weeks on T.V. When I came into the room, the two of them waved the paper at me. The friend wanted my pen so Mario could sign the contract. Wanted to know how soon he could begin singing again."

"And he won't ever sing . . ." Kathy shook her head. "Didn't his doctor explain to him before the operation?"

"Maybe. Maybe not. If he did, it probably was in English. Mario doesn't understand much English. He came from Mexico when he was a kid. He didn't go to school. He followed the crops."

Kathy understood what that meant. From harvesting sugar beets or lettuce in the Imperial Valley, up through the Central Coast for carrots or 'cots or berries, from picking cotton in Kern County to tomatoes in the Sacramento Delta or melons in the San Joaquin Valley, migrant workers went from job to job, a week here, a month there. Few of them had a chance to go to school or to learn English if it was not their native tongue.

"I looked at the paper," Jenny went on. "And, Kathy, do you know who he is? He's Mario Ferraro. You remember when we used to stop for sodas and play the juke box over near Benita Street?"

"Those Mexican songs Gail was so nuts about?"

Jenny nodded. "My patient made those records. He won't ever make any more. I guess I looked kind of funny, because the guitar player beckoned me outside. I let him have it. Straight. For a minute he didn't say a word. Then he said, real slowly, '*El hambre. Sabe tener hambre?* Do you know hunger? Not to be hungry for a meal for a day, but to be hungry all the time? We've gone hungry waiting for this break,' he said, 'because Mario's voice was worth it.' "

"But they must have made a lot of records. There were several in that one juke box," Kathy interrupted.

"They weren't paid anything. A man backed them— an agent. Said he'd build them up and get them on T.V., and he did. 'You'll have to tell Mario,' I said to the guitar player and he just looked at me and broke his guitar over his knee and walked out into the street. And there I was, with Mario."

"What did you do, Jenny? Did you tell Mario the truth?"

"How could I until I had consulted the doctor?"

"But later?"

"Yes, I told him, this morning. He'll follow the crops for the rest of his life."

"Isn't there *anything* you could do, Jenny?"

Jenny smiled, a little sadly. "You can't imagine feeling sorry for somebody and not being able to do anything about it, can you, Kathy?"

"Yes, I can," Kathy answered. She wasn't thinking of the Mexican singer who wouldn't sing again, but of Collin Monroe, her patient at Ocean Cliff. Of course, he wasn't her patient any more.

Kathy was sure that Collin was suffering from a sense of guilt because he had been the driver of the car in which Edwin Maxfield was killed. Mrs. Smith, the head nurse, had been inclined to agree, when she had seen the newspaper clipping, that the boy had learned of Edwin Maxfield's death. But the doctor's orders were still to refrain from talking about the accident, at least until Collin's fever subsided. And for the last two days of Kathy's stay at Ocean Cliff, Collin had been kept under sedation. She had had no opportunity to talk with him again. It was a relief, nevertheless, to talk about it to Jenny and to have her friend agree that it might have helped if the boy could or would have talked.

"If patients just didn't have feelings and problems to get in the way of recovery, nursing would be easy," Jenny said. "But our jobs would be as dull as taking care of Mary Chase, and about as meaningful."

"That poor dummy!" Kathy smiled. "Remember all the needle pricks in her plastic rump?"

"Better hers than mine," Jenny said. "But Mrs. Seaforth took almost as many hypos as Mary Chase." The girls were still grateful to the brave Nursing Arts instructor who had let the whole class give her practice shots.

The canyon had given way to green vineyards and open fields, and then to the palm-lined streets of Sacramento. There was a stop for lunch in the grimy bus station and then the crowded bus ground its gears and climbed.

The two girls were entranced by the towering forests of pine and redwood and the cool ripple of the broad river. Late afternoon brought them a flag stop at Rough and Ready, California, a glimpse of Lake Tahoe, gleaming blue, far below the highway, and then, half buried in a jumble of roadside billboards, a battered sign that said *State Line*.

It was dusk when the bus drew up at a poorly lighted filling station at the edge of the woods. The driver turned half around. "Didn't you girls say you wanted off at Silver Spoon Junction?" he said. "This is it."

Before Kathy had their bags off the rack, Gail and Kelley and Yo were hopping up and down outside and tapping at the window.

"The town's on the side road, part way up the mountain. All five buildings of it!" Gail explained as the bus pulled away.

A broad-shouldered, red-headed young man sauntered over and reached for the suitcases by the roadside.

"Sean," Gail said. "Meet Kathy Martin and Jenny Ramirez. Now you know the whole bunch! Sean is my cousin," she added. "He's one of the ushers."

"And he's done nothing but sit under a tree and sing sad songs since he heard that Steve wasn't coming with you to protect him from five females of the nursing profession," Kelley interjected.

"Do you sing professionally?" Jenny asked.

"I'm a professional monotone. I just sing to drown out my guitar," the young man answered drily.

"Sean's a mining engineer," Gail said. "He's mapped out a tour of ghost towns for Matt and me to explore on our honeymoon. And don't let Kelley fool you, Jenny. He knows his luck at having the field to himself with Matt and his other two ushers not getting in till tomorrow. Jim Telford's coming, by the way. Orders from Linda, so she'll be represented at the wedding."

"Who is Matt's fourth usher?" Kathy asked. Steve had wondered.

"Didn't I write you? Jake Golden, the photographer on the paper. The one who gets to take the 'X marks the spot' pictures for Matt's police items."

Christopher Matthews had a master's degree in journalism, but his job on the San Francisco paper was police reporter. This was scarcely what he had hoped for. Still, he and Gail considered themselves lucky because they could start housekeeping in San Francisco. And Gail was sure that his talent for writing would be recognized at any moment.

Sean led the way to a battered station wagon. As they piled into the car, Kathy noticed that he maneuvered Jenny into the front seat beside him, and that Jenny, usually so shy with strangers, was talking a mile a minute.

Yo caught Kathy's eye and whispered delightedly, "Music! It's the one subject that could have done it."

The lively conversation continued through the ride to the Hendersons' house. Supper was barely finished before Sean brought out his guitar. As the moon rose over the mountain top, the whole crowd sat on the front porch and sang—all but Gail's five-year-old sister, Sue.

"She's catching up on her beauty sleep," Mrs. Henderson said. "She's been going to bed at seven like a lamb ever since Gail said she could be the flower girl."

The wedding was to be at home, in the parlor of the rambling old house. Gail's sister Nancy, who was going to nursing school next year, was to be maid of honor, and Matt had asked George, Gail's brother, just turned seventeen, to be his best man.

"Too bad Matt's family lives so far away," Mrs. Henderson murmured. "I can't get over not having them."

"There are so many Hendersons in the wedding party," Gail's father teased, "there won't be anybody to see the show."

"Nobody but the whole population for twenty miles around," Gail answered. "Besides any strangers in town that Dad happens to run into."

"That reminds me!" Mr. Henderson had been standing in the doorway. Now he ducked inside and in a few moments Mrs. Henderson followed. Then George disappeared. Sounds came from the parlor.

"I do believe they're waxing that floor again!" Gail murmured affectionately. "It's a good thing we don't have a wedding every day. Sing *Cielito Lindo*, Jenny. Then we'll go up and try on our dresses."

But Jenny and Sean were still singing duets when the others trooped upstairs. An hour passed with talk of clothes and presents and honeymoon plans.

"Blue jeans and a flannel shirt will make a slightly peculiar going-away costume," Gail was saying, when a furious barking of dogs interrupted.

A car was coming up the driveway. *Steve?* Kathy ran to the window hopefully. Maybe the fire at Cromwell hadn't been out of control after all.

"It's Matt!" Jenny's voice came out of the darkness. "And Jim and somebody else."

"Hey, Gail!" Sean shouted. "Here's the bridegroom in person. Thought he wasn't coming till tomorrow."

The girls came clattering down the stairs to the porch.

"I got off at noon and drove straight through," Matt was saying. "Where's Gail? I've got something to tell her!"

Gail and Matt disappeared into the kitchen, leaving the others on the front steps, slightly bewildered and apprehensive. To Kathy it seemed that Matt appeared excited but worried.

"Is anything wrong?" she asked Jim Telford.

"Not to my way of thinking," Jim answered. "You tell it, Jake," he said to the stranger. "Oh, you haven't met these girls yet, have you?"

"What's the scoop?" Kelley asked impatiently as introductions were completed.

"It's the honeymoon," Jake Golden answered. "This morning a hot tip came into the paper and the chief offered Matt the chance to follow it up. It could be a big assignment. Tracking down a counterfeiting operation, or what may be a counterfeiting operation. Might mean a by-line for Matt and all."

"But won't it wait till after the honeymoon?" Kathy put in.

"That's just it. No honeymoon in the ghost towns. Seems they've been planning the trip for months. But not ever having had a honeymoon myself," he added, "nor seen a ghost town either, I don't dig Matt's worry."

"Gail has been looking forward to the trip," Jenny said. "She loves exploring. Still and all, ghost towns don't disappear—and counterfeiters might."

"Counterfeit gang." Kelley frowned. "Sounds kind of dangerous."

Jake shrugged. "Matt doesn't strike me as a timid guy. I don't know much about the assignment except that Matt's keen on it. But I expect one doesn't like to disappoint the bride—at least not before the wedding."

"Hey, kids!" Gail's voice came from the kitchen. "Come on and help us raid the icebox!"

Her eyes were sparkling when they trooped into the kitchen.

"Did Jake tell you?" she asked, all her Sherlock Holmes instincts to the fore.

"You're going to give up your camping trip?" Yo asked, thinking of the suitcase full of lovely sports clothes she had helped pack that afternoon.

Mrs. Henderson appeared in the doorway before Gail could answer. "You don't have to make up your minds tonight," she said, when the dilemma had been explained to her. "Get some food. Gail, there's turkey and ham and that coconut cake. These boys must be starved after riding half the night. Then Sean will take the men off to his cabin, won't you, Sean?" She smiled and patted Matt's hand. "There's a wedding tomorrow morning, if you remember. You don't want Gail yawning when she says 'I do.' Besides, it's long after midnight and the bridegroom isn't supposed to see the bride on their wedding day!"

VI

"My Heart Is Like a Singing Bird"

"Something old, something new," chanted Sue at the breakfast table next morning.

"Something borrowed—that's mother's wedding handkerchief," Gail said.

"Something blue," Sue shouted triumphantly, waving her cereal spoon perilously in the air.

"Something blue?" Kelley poured her second cup of coffee. "You can wear Kathy if Steve doesn't show up pretty soon."

Kathy heaved a sigh. She *was* worried. It was almost eleven o'clock and she'd been listening for the sound of Steve's car since dawn. Suppose the fire in the park had turned out to be so bad that Steve couldn't leave? Suppose he was hurt and in some hospital, overcome by smoke. Or with a broken shoulder, like that time at the

Big Basin fire—or suppose he'd started last night and fallen asleep at the wheel and . . . She refused to finish that thought. She shuddered, remembering the sight of Collin Monroe's body hurtling to the pavement on the mountain road. The Santa Cruz mountains were just anthills compared to these Sierra Nevada giants.

The phone rang and Kathy knocked over her chair in her haste to answer.

"It's for you, Ramirez," she said as she returned to the table. "It's Sean," she whispered, when Jenny had left the room. "Wanted to know if there was any reason he couldn't take Jenny for a walk—even if the bride was incommunicado."

"You're going of course!" the others chorused when Jenny reappeared, trying to look as if she was accustomed to being besieged for dates by attractive young men with red hair and a guitar.

"Is it all right?" she asked Mrs. Henderson. "Don't you need me to help? I'm pretty good in the kitchen, you know."

"There's nothing to do," Mrs. Henderson lied cheerfully.

"Now, Mrs. Henderson, give us all jobs!" Yo said, when Jenny was safely out of the door. "I'll clear up the breakfast dishes. Gail can moon over her cold coffee in the kitchen."

Gail jumped at the sound of her name. She'd hardly spoken a word all morning. "I was thinking about the counterfeiters," she said. "Do you suppose they specialize in coins or greenbacks? Can't you see the headlines: *Cub Reporter Captures Shrewd Gang Unaided?*"

Kelley laughed. "You're a charming bride-to-be, Henderson, but as a journalist you get a C minus. Try again."

" *'I Owe It All to My Wife,' Says Star Sleuth after Capture of Counterfeit Gang!*" Kathy suggested. "I take it you've decided to abandon the ghost towns."

"What are a few ghosts compared to a gang of counterfeiters?" Gail said. She glanced at her watch and leapt out of her chair as if she had sighted either a ghost or a counterfeiter.

"What's wrong with her?" Yo said, as Gail went dashing up the stairs.

"Bridal jitters, maybe? In two hours she'll be Mrs. Christopher Matthews, you know," Kelley suggested.

"Listen!" Mrs. Henderson was standing at the kitchen door, her head cocked to one side. "I hear a car. It might be my husband and George. They went to town to get the cake. No, it's not the station wagon," she added after a moment. "It's coming from the south."

Kathy made a dash for the window.

"Looks like we'll have a fourth usher, after all," Kelley remarked as Steve's red convertible swung into the drive.

"And all in one piece!" Kathy murmured.

She followed the others to the porch, a broad smile on her face. It wouldn't do to let Steve know how worried she'd been. When the greetings were over, Steve went back to his car and hauled out a huge white box, the kind florists use.

"Mrs. Martin stripped her garden. She doesn't think flowers grow outside of California," he said.

Mrs. Henderson flushed with pleasure and held out her arms for the box. "Your mother must be a mind reader, Kathy! Matt had to order the bride's bouquet sent air express from San Francisco. Except for my zinnia patch there's not a blossom on the mountain in September!"

"Where's Gail?" Steve said, fishing in his capacious jacket pocket. "I've got a present for her—not exactly a wedding present . . ."

Kathy looked around. Where *was* Gail? She couldn't still be talking to Matt on the telephone . . .

Steve's hand came out triumphantly. Curled up in his broad, brown palm, with only its pert nose and perkier ears sticking up, was a three-week-old puppy.

"Oh, the darling! Can I hold it? What's its name?" Sue danced up and down in rapture.

"Don't squeeze the pup too tight," Mrs. Henderson warned. "He's just a baby, Sue. A Dalmatian, isn't he?" she asked Steve. "A firehouse dog. They're charming. Gail will be pleased."

"Where is Gail?" Steve repeated.

"Let's find her, quick!" shouted Sue.

There was a rush for the stairs. Kathy fell a little behind with Steve. It was the first chance she'd had to speak to him.

"I'm so glad you made it," she said a little tremulously.

"Did you think I'd miss the chance to dance with my

girl at a wedding? And to see you in that dress you were so busy stitching?"

"The girls like it, Steve. We tried on our dresses last night—and Kelley has made dreamy little caps with veils —she just twisted some velvet ribbon around pipe cleaners—the color of hickory leaves in the fall with the sun shining through—the velvet I mean, not the pipe cleaners—Whatever is Gail up to?"

They had come to the door of Gail's little room. She was kneeling on the floor, pawing like a squirrel through an open suitcase. Out came blue jeans, old sweaters and hiking boots—in went red-heeled pumps, white gloves and a lacy blouse rescued just in time from the puppy who had wiggled out of Susan's arms.

Yo groaned, "I packed everything so beautifully!"

"But only what the well-dressed bride wears in ghost towns," Kelley said. "Can't you see? The honeymoon's off! Here, let me help—you'll never get that suitcase closed, the way you're going about it!"

"Thanks, Jonesy. I guess I'm a little excited." Gail gathered the puppy in her arms. She was radiant with happiness and looked lovely even in rumpled slacks and with her pale blond hair done up in curlers.

"Hi, Steve! I adore the pup. Matt always said the first thing we would need to start housekeeping with was a dog! Did Kathy tell you? We're going straight to our new apartment tomorrow! Matt has a terrifically important assignment. Strictly hush-hush. We just established a branch of the Do-It-Yourself Detective Agency. Mr. and

Mrs. Sherlock Holmes and—" she tweaked the puppy's ear, "the newest member, Perry Mason Junior."

"Is *that* his name?" Sue raced downstairs to spread the news. They could hear her chanting through the hall. "Ma, the puppy's name is Merry, Merry—something—"

"Merry you are!" Gail held the dog at arm's length to admire him. "See that you come, sir, when your master calls."

Kelley had begun to bring order out of the chaos on the floor. "Hang a 'No Visitors' sign on this door," she commanded, "until I get this packing done. And take Merry with you. I've got a scatterbrained bride and a D.I. suitcase on my hands."

"Certainly, nurse," Yo said in her most professional tone. "We'll give Mrs. Henderson a hand."

Obediently, Kathy and Steve followed Yo down the stairs.

"The ceremony's going to take place in the parlor," Kathy explained to Steve. "Matt will come in from the back room—and we'll come down the stairs and through the archway—there where the screen is. Then we'll march out each one on the arm of an usher—across the hall to the dining room where the bride's table will be. Like this!" she added, pulling him through the dining room and into the kitchen.

It looked like a bargain day on Market Street, but that was because so many people were busy with so many things. Jenny and Sean had returned, and Jenny was helping Nancy pack a huge hamper of food. Sean lolled in the doorway and gave directions, such as "Don't forget the bread and butter pickles" and "Don't skimp on the chocolate cake."

Mrs. Henderson had a row of vases lined up and her hands full of flowers. She gratefully turned them over to Yo.

"I thought we'd have to make do with potted ferns. Now the room is going to be a flower garden. I'm so grateful to you, Steve, for bringing them. Who'd have thought to see delphinium and heliotrope in September! And chrysanthemums as big as cabbages! You fix 'em, Yo. Any way you like."

"What do you want kept out for the parlor?" Yo asked.

"Not a thing!" It was Mr. Henderson who answered. He and George had just come in, loaded with packages.

"Cake—three tiers high," he said. "Minnie Winona at the bakery did herself proud. And the post office is going to shut up an hour early so everybody there can come to the wedding." Gail's father was clearly enjoying all the bustle and fuss. Kathy had hardly noticed him last night. She saw now where Gail's zest came from. His eyes were as blue as Gail's, too—with the same twinkle. George was more like their mother—serious-eyed behind his spectacles and weighted with the responsibility of being best man at his sister's wedding.

"Here's the package from the express station. What do I do with it, Mom? Take it up to Sis?"

"Heavens, no! It's the bridal bouquets!" Mrs. Henderson was busy packing a hamper. "Put the box in the refrigerator, son," she said. "And bring out the fried chicken while you're there." She looked up helplessly at Steve. "The clock goes round so fast—twelve-thirty already—I'm fixing a snack for you boys. Sean and George will take you up to the cabin."

"You're Steve, aren't you?" George shook hands with Steve a little shyly.

"George is Matt's best man," Kathy explained, "and Nancy's the maid of honor."

Nancy had been working quietly, steadily, all morning without getting any notice. She looked up gratefully when Kathy mentioned her name and then fastened her eyes again on the butter spreader.

"I'd like a job, Mrs. Henderson," Kathy said.

"Well, now, let's see . . . The bride's table is all set, the punch is made—all but the ice and sparkling water. There's our lunch, but that can wait till the men folks are out of the way. I'll tell you what you do!" Mrs. Henderson was plainly pleased with her solution. "You take that young man who's been driving all night out on the front porch and give him a glass of lemonade!"

"Slave driver, isn't she?" Kathy stretched out luxuriously in a redwood lounge chair.

"I'm going to recommend Mrs. Henderson for the diplomatic corps," Steve answered. "How did she know I wanted to see you alone?"

Kathy sat up straight as a ramrod. "Is something wrong? Somebody's sick at home! My orders have come for Alaska!"

Steve laughed, "There you go! The world's best worrier." He pulled a letter out of his pocket. "Your mother wanted me to wait until after the wedding to give you this letter from Ocean Cliff. But you're not a child. You've got what it takes—and after all, the letter may be just a bill for laundry!"

"It may be from Collin. Maybe he's better."

Kathy deliberately put any other possibility from her mind. Nevertheless her hand trembled as she tore the flap on the envelope and unfolded the typewritten sheet.

She scanned the single sentence hurriedly. "Hey, Steve! They want me back. More vacations coming up and they'll arrange for me to take the Red Cross course I need in Monterey!"

"Is that good news?" Steve looked a little crestfallen. "After all, you're going to be gone a whole year, in Alaska."

"But, Steve, you're down the coast a lot. And I'll have Collin for a patient! I'm sure I can do him some good."

If Steve was disappointed, he hid it. Kathy was wholly a nurse again. Without hope of carrying them out, she had made all sorts of plans for getting through to her patient. Maybe they had come to accept her theory at the hospital—that the boy's physical setback came from a feeling of guilt at having caused the death of his friend.

"Anyway, they must have liked my work," she said, "or they wouldn't have asked me back again!"

She folded the letter and tucked it in her pocket a little complacently.

"There's Sean calling you! I wish you didn't have to go, Steve. I'd like to talk about how to get through to a patient and restore his confidence. I wish I knew more—about psychology I mean."

"I thought you said you were through with learning."

"Now you're teasing. You wouldn't like me, would you, if I didn't care about being as good a nurse as I can?"

"I like you plenty." Steve came over and sat on the arm of her chair.

"There's Sean calling again!" Kathy said hurriedly. "He's nice. You'll like him. And Steve, something perfectly dreamy—we all think he's falling for Jenny!"

"I hear that weddings are catching, like the measles," he said with a half-smile on his face—and then he was gone.

Would I give up Alaska if he asked me to? Kathy wondered. At this moment she could not honestly say.

"But it's just the wedding, Kathy Martin," she told herself. "Everybody gets romantic at weddings. Tomorrow I'm going to make a careful plan for getting through to my patient in Room 202, Ocean Cliff Hospital. I'll present it to the head nurse, and if she isn't interested, I'll carry it out by myself!"

It was four o'clock to the minute when the first notes of Mendelssohn's *Wedding March* sounded from the piano in the dining room. Upstairs in her room, surrounded by her bridesmaids, Gail giggled nervously.

"Just in time," she said. "Cousin Kate has played her whole repertoire."

They had been dressed for hours, it seemed, looking out of the window at the guests pouring in. The early ones had all carried trays of food.

"The neighbors," Mrs. Henderson had explained. "Everybody wanted to make something for the reception. It's like that with us in the country. Weddings and funerals and moving days—you know what it means to be a neighbor."

Then she'd given a last twitch to Gail's veil, and put the old-fashioned bouquet of tiny white rosebuds and maidenhair fern in her daughter's hands. She'd stood for a moment in the doorway, then, choked up with love and pride, had run down to receive the guests, leaving the girls alone.

"Why was Mama blowing her nose?" Sue wanted to know.

Nobody could tell Sue why mothers cry at weddings, unless, Kathy said, it was because brides look so special.

Gail's dress was a white sheath of the same raw silk Kelley had chosen for the bridesmaids. Over the skirt, gossamer organza floated like a fleecy cloud, and the veil was of lace that Mrs. Henderson's mother had brought across the mountains in a covered wagon almost a hundred years ago.

Something old, something new, something borrowed —Mrs. Henderson's best handkerchief—and something blue. The "something blue" was a pin set with tiny sapphires just the color of Gail's eyes. That was Matt's gift to his bride.

The *Wedding March* had been played through once when Mrs. Henderson appeared in the doorway. It was time for the procession to begin. Yo started down the stairs, followed by Jenny, cradling long-stemmed chrysanthemums. Kelley was next, then Kathy, just ahead of Nancy. Nancy's dress was green tulle. Kathy was aware of the swish of little Sue's starched muslin and an encouraging whisper as someone put a basket of flowers in the child's hands at the foot of the stairs.

Kathy caught her breath with surprise. The big old parlor that had seemed rather bare last night was transformed. White ribbons made an aisle to the bay window. And the bay had become a woodland glade of vines and mosses and ferns just as they grew in the forest. That was what Mr. Henderson and George had been up to! Kathy's eyes searched out Steve, taller than the other ushers. She would stand just in front of him in the half circle.

The minister was a shriveled little man in a coat too large for him. He was almost lost among the ferns. He was an old friend and had known Gail's mother since her childhood.

Here comes the bride. Gail was down the stairs now. She came forward solemnly, on the arm of her father. But when Matt stepped out of the circle to meet her, she flashed him a smile.

That smile was what Kathy remembered long afterward whenever she thought of Gail's wedding. The ceremony, the gay crowded reception, Jenny catching the

bride's bouquet, throwing rice and old shoes when "Mr. and Mrs. Christopher Matthews" drove off toward San Francisco—all these were like any other wedding. It was fun being a bridesmaid. But Gail's smile was like a poem by Christina Rossetti that Kathy had once read in the school library. Back in San Tomás, before going to Ocean Cliff, she copied out the verse for her scrapbook:

> *My heart is like a singing bird*
> *Whose nest is in a watered shoot;*
> *My heart is like an apple tree*
> *Whose boughs are bent with thickset fruit;*
> *My heart is like a rainbow shell*
> *That paddles in a halcyon sea;*
> *My heart is gladder than all these*
> *Because my love is come to me.*

VII

Old Mother Hubbard

"Miss Martin! You really did come back!" Sally ran to open the door for Kathy with a worshipful "I'm-going-to-be-a-nurse-too" look in her eyes. "I do like San Tomás caps," she added. "They're the most, really too much. Of course, they won't look as scrumptious on me. I just bet your hair is naturally curly!"

"Too curly down here at the coast," Kathy answered. "How are my patients?"

She really meant, "How is Collin?" A plan all written out to give Mrs. Smith was tucked in her apron pocket. In her few days at home after the wedding, she had read a big, fat book on the effects of emotional disturbance on the body.

Sally giggled. "They aren't here yet—your patients, I mean. Didn't anybody write you? You're supposed to go

79

on duty in the maternity wing. I'm not sure if it'll be nursery or labor room, really."

"Maternity wing?" It took Kathy a moment to digest the news of her new assignment. "What about—" *No use asking about Collin,* she thought, stopping short. She tried to hide her disappointment.

Sally obviously had not noticed anything. She chattered gaily on about the maternity wing. "There've been more babies born this week than there are clams on the beach," she said. "Old Mother Hubbard will sure be glad to see you."

"Old *who?*"

Sally retreated to her desk. "Oh, excuse me, Miss Martin. I shouldn't have called her that—not to an R.N. Miss Hubbard, I meant to say. The head nurse in Maternity. All the aides call her—what I said."

Kathy glanced at the clock above Sally's desk. Almost three o'clock! She looked wistfully toward the medical-surgical wing. Was there time for a swift glance at Room 202? Just to see if Collin . . . ?

"Are you the relief nurse?"

At the question, Kathy swung around. A lean, stoop-shouldered woman in white uniform gazed at her from behind old-fashioned, steel-rimmed spectacles.

"I'm Kathy Martin. You're Miss Hubbard, aren't you?"

The woman's eyes traveled from the tip of Kathy's white shoes to the black stripe on her cap. "So you're the nurse Mrs. Smith recommended so highly? Perhaps on *Medical,* youth is no drawback."

When Kathy was talked to in that tone of voice, she usually became acutely conscious of her height. Before the head nurse of the maternity ward, she felt suddenly like the gawky high-school girl she had been a half-dozen years before.

"I suppose, Miss Martin, you had the usual six weeks in O.B. at nursing school?"

Kathy answered in a small voice, "My senior service was in the nursery."

"Hmph." Miss Hubbard sighed. "Well, it's only for a week. One manages, somehow. But every year, they get younger and younger."

Next thing, she'll ask if I can read and write, Kathy thought as she followed the older woman to the nurse's station on the obstetrical ward.

Miss Hubbard scowled down at her charts. "I suppose you have some knowledge of the stages of labor. But you youngsters never can tell the difference between a whiner and a patient ready to deliver . . ."

I'll be happy to leave if you don't want me here. Kathy never said it, but the words were on the tip of her tongue a hundred times during the next few evenings.

To Kathy, it appeared that the original Old Mother Hubbard showed more sympathy for her dog than this one for her patients. She was gruff and businesslike with the young mothers, while Kathy's training called for gentle sympathy. She scolded Kathy for spending extra time with one patient or another, insisted that charts be kept to a T, discouraged Kathy from calling the doctors. And above all, she continued to be scornful of "book learning," of young nurses, and indeed, of the medical profession as a whole, when it came to the process of having babies.

Originally, Kathy learned, Miss Hubbard had come from England, and there she had been a professional midwife. Kathy had a great respect for the practice of obstetrics in England, for at nursing school she had been required to read Dr. Read's *Childbirth without Fear.* But Miss Hubbard pooh-poohed Dr. Read, and said that all this commotion about natural childbirth was ridiculous.

"Nothing unnatural about childbirth in the first place," she said, "until the doctors made all the fuss."

One day Kathy proudly spoke of a patient who had delivered her baby without need of sedatives or anesthesia. She had attended natural childbirth classes, and her husband stayed with her until it was time to go to the delivery room. Kathy had gone into Delivery, as she often had to do, and couldn't stop talking about the cooperativeness of her patient, and how easily she had given birth.

"Of course," she said, "not all the mothers who take the childbirth classes come through with flying colors."

"Classes! These youngsters nowadays have to be taught every single thing," Miss Hubbard said scornfully. "If there were a few more competent nurses, they wouldn't need classes at all."

"How do you mean, Miss Hubbard?" Kathy asked. "Don't you think the training helps them?"

"No better than a nurse can. *If* she knows what to do."

But Miss Hubbard seemed to have no interest in teaching Kathy what to do—if indeed she knew. The young mothers, often just out of their teens, with no idea what to expect, were the ones that gave Kathy the most trouble. As often as she had time, she would stop, talk with them, hold their hands, rub their backs, and sometimes try to explain to them what was going on inside their bodies. Nothing seemed to do much good, however, once they let themselves get frightened. That was why she was so glad to have patients who knew the processes of childbirth, the need to relax, and how to relax.

She had to admit that somehow, in her gruff, unpleasant way, Mother Hubbard managed to keep patients comparatively quiet.

"I think she scares the patients worse than the mysteries of childbirth," she said to Nadine Gregory one night. "That's why they're so quiet when she's around."

"Don't kid yourself," Nadine answered. "Old Mother Hubbard really knows her stuff. If you get a chance, watch her in operation. I know it's hard when you're both so busy, but I certainly learned a lot working with her when I was in O.B."

Kathy shook her head doubtfully. She had three days to go in Maternity, and she could hardly wait for them to be over. "How can I watch her when she snarls every time I get within earshot?"

"Well, stick with her, and don't let that fierce manner fool you. It's just the way she is with new girls."

The news from Room 202 added to Kathy's woes. Collin Monroe, who had earned the reputation of being the pest of the medical-surgical wing, was showing no improvement at all. Laboratory tests went on almost every day, but so far, the doctors had been unable to find any organic reason why the boy's bones should not heal at a normal rate. Kathy had been in to see Collin twice just before work. Both times he had been under sedation and too sleepy to talk. She had tried to see Mrs. Smith about her plan for "getting through" to Collin, but Mrs. Smith had been swamped with work and had put Kathy off with a kindly remark about appreciating her interest in her former patients.

She was leaving the hospital on Wednesday night when Sally called to her from the desk.

"What is it, Sally?" Kathy knew she sounded rude and unfriendly, but she couldn't face another session of Sally's chatter.

"You're—you're tired, aren't you?" The hurt was evident in Sally's voice.

"I'm beat to the socks, drug down, and long gone," Kathy said, forcing a smile.

No need to take out her bad temper on worshipful little Sally. "Too much Mother Hubbard, I guess. But I do have to get to bed."

"Yes, of course. I won't keep you. You have a letter that came this afternoon. I didn't have a chance to bring it to you."

Sally trotted around the desk with an envelope. Kathy

grinned at the return address: Mrs. Christopher Matthews, written in Gail's clear script.

Kathy flopped down on the hospital lawn and tore open the envelope. A leaflet fluttered to the grass. A catalog from the Edwin Maxfield memorial show. Kathy stuck the catalog in her pocket and fished for Gail's letter. It was short, but happiness bubbled in every line.

Dear Martin,

Nobody ever had such bridesmaids! The coffee table was waiting for us when we walked into the apartment. (No, Matt did not carry me over the threshold—he carried Merry!) The table is simply beautiful and I suppose you know that Yo had slipped in and arranged a bowl of chrysanthemums on it, and had coffee perking on the two-burner stove. How she timed our arrival from our "wedding trip" of one night at Lake Tahoe, we'll never know.

Matt and I are spending heavenly days at galleries—in the line of duty. I can't tell you much about his assignment—it's very private-eye—until we get the goods on the villains. But Matt said to tell you to forget our vision of a non-governmental mint near the Golden Gate! The counterfeit deal is definitely not greenbacks.

Come soon to have coffee on our most beautiful—and only—piece of furniture.

Love,
Gail

P.S. We have just bestowed the degree of R.N. on the pup. (Royal Nitwit)—but of course he and I haven't taken our State Boards yet.

Kathy looked at the art gallery catalog. Perhaps this would interest Collin, now that the doctor had rescinded the order about not discussing Maxfield. Collin would surely be pleased about the memorial exhibit. She decided to come in early once more to see him.

Collin never saw the catalog. When Kathy went into the room the next day, he opened up with a tirade against Kathy for walking out on him, against the doctors and nurses for conspiring to keep him trapped in a plaster cast, against the human race in general for "not giving a hoot what happened to him." Before Kathy could get a word in edgewise, the day nurse came in with his medication and looked at Kathy with such a cold glare that she fled to the cafeteria for a cup of coffee.

Kathy had no opportunity to study Miss Hubbard's methods when she went to work. She had barely reached the O.B. desk when the phone rang. Miss Hubbard's clipped voice grated on her ears.

"Miss Martin? I will be unavoidably detained tonight. It may be six or seven this evening before I reach the hospital. Ask Mrs. Anderson to stay on with you if possible. Call Mrs. Smith if you need her." A brief discussion of the patients in labor, a few orders rattled off at top speed, and down went the telephone at the other end with a bang.

"Did she say what time she would be in?" asked the day-shift floor nurse when Kathy explained the situation.

"She said it might be six or seven o'clock, Mrs. Anderson. Can you stay?"

The older woman shook her head. "Not past five. My husband will be here to pick me up then. But things aren't too busy, so I'm sure you'll be able to manage for that hour."

Kathy didn't feel so awfully sure, but she was determined not to show her lack of confidence.

"That will be fine," she said cheerfully. "How is Mrs. Browning in 11-A coming along? She came in late last night, just before midnight."

"She's in Delivery now. In fact, they're probably about ready for the Nursery nurse. Will you check?"

Kathy started toward Delivery but before she got to the door, the sound of a newborn baby's cry reached her ears, and she turned back to telephone the nursery.

"Come and get your new patient, Annette!" she said to the answering voice.

Whatever the problems of O.B. nursing, this was a happy moment not only for the families of patients, but for all the staff. Whoever had a hand in seeing maternity patients through delivery somehow felt a personal pride and joy in the birth of a new baby.

Kathy walked over to the delivery room and stuck her head in the door. "Boy or girl?"

"Girl. Everything fine. You can tell the father."

With a smile Kathy turned toward the fathers' waiting room. Only one man was there—harassed, rumpled-haired, wearing the same helpless, father-to-be look that has been caricatured for unknown ages.

"Mr. Browning?"

The young man jumped a foot and turned a frightened face toward Kathy.

"Everything is fine. You have a beautiful little daughter, and your wife is feeling wonderful. They'll be bringing her and the baby by in a few minutes. Would you like to step out in the hall and wait?"

The harassed look faded and a broad smile covered young Mr. Browning's freckled face.

"Deborah Ann Browning—that's what we're going to name her! We've had a boy's name and a girl's name picked out for six months. Deborah Ann. Do you think that's a good name?"

"Very nice. You come out here and wait now. They'll be out in a minute."

The other patients in labor—three of them—were progressing slowly. All had been admitted since noon. At five o'clock, when Mrs. Anderson left, things were calm and under control. At five-thirty, Kathy was in the process of admitting a new patient—a woman of about thirty-five who already had three children. At five-thirty-five a cry of "Nurse! Nurse!" came from the patient in 12-B. Kathy left one of the aides to finish admitting the new patient and went to Mrs. Jackson in 12-B. At five-thirty-seven, the young girl in 13-A began to fuss. Kathy ran in to see her, stethoscope in hand. She examined the patient and checked the unborn baby's heartbeat. The mother-to-be relaxed nicely while Kathy was in the room, but the moment she left, her nervous cries began again. By five-forty-five, the tension had proved catching, and Kathy found herself rushing from room to room, comforting, hand-holding, examining. The only patient who seemed to be calm was the one latest admitted—Mrs. Ames in 14-A.

At six o'clock Kathy was completely exhausted. There was no sign of Old Mother Hubbard. The patients continued to demand attention without respite. Only Mrs. Ames was quiet.

At six-fifteen the signal light over the door of 14-A flashed on. *That*, thought Kathy, *makes it unanimous*. She started toward 14-A, only to be stopped by the patient in room 11-B. A quick examination made her decide to call Mrs. Jackson's doctor. She ran for the phone, when the patient in 14-A called rather urgently. Kathy paused, halfway to the telephone. She stifled an impulse to howl for help herself.

"Call Jackson's doctor, and prepare a delivery room," she directed the aide. "I'd better see what 14-A wants."

Kathy bit her tongue. She had vowed never to think of patients as room numbers instead of as people. As she ran down the hall every signal light was on. Calls of "Nurse!" from 11 and 12. Groans from 13. Only 14 was quiet, but she suddenly realized that she hadn't been near Mrs. Ames in the last half-hour. And a fourth child can be born quickly!

A moment later Kathy rushed out of 14 and almost bumped into Miss Hubbard.

"I think we're about to have two deliveries at once," she gasped.

"It happens," Miss Hubbard said with a ghost of a smile. "Is 11-B one of them? I saw Mrs. Jackson's doctor arriving."

Kathy nodded. "And this one," she said, pointing to room 14. "She's only been in for an hour."

Miss Hubbard turned swiftly. "Carrie Ames, no doubt. She waits till the last minute every time. You take Mrs. Jackson. I'll handle the rest of the patients."

Things were calm and peaceful by the end of the shift, and Kathy prepared her charts to give to the night nurse.

Miss Hubbard passed by the desk on the way to the nursery. She put her hand lightly on Kathy's shoulder.

"For an inexperienced girl, you did very well."

Kathy turned red as a beet. "I was awful, Miss Hubbard. I was about ready to scream when you showed up. How on earth did you quiet things down so quickly?"

"I just showed the young ones how to breathe and relax. A little reassurance goes a long way," the older woman answered.

"Do you think I could learn?" Kathy asked humbly.

"Not everything at once. But I can give you some pointers. That is," she added with a twinkle, "if you don't mind taking lessons from Old Mother Hubbard."

VIII

A Date with Steve

Kathy's day off, after her grueling week in O.B., was spent lazily at home. Steve was away on some kind of conference in San Tomás. Nick drove her back to her job in a ten-year-old car he had tinkered back to life. His own car, for college!

"She runs sweet," he gloated, "even on these hills. And around Davis the roads are flat as a mill pond."

They had passed through Monterey and Carmel, and were in the Big Sur Canyon, rounding curves, with the ocean roaring and swirling fifty feet below. Another mile and the lights of the hospital would come into sight. Kathy's thoughts leaped ahead. Tomorrow morning she'd go back to the Medical Wing. Day shift. Her roommate Nadine Gregory was going on her vacation. This would be her time—if ever—to get through to Collin Monroe.

"How would *you* feel, Nick, if you had an accident and your passenger was killed?"

"For crying out loud!" Nick was thoroughly aggrieved. "Just because this old bus isn't the latest model is no reason to go imagining things!"

Kathy snuggled down in her seat. "I didn't mean it that way, stupid. You're a wonderful driver—but you're just about the age of my patient. . . ."

"Thought you had a floor full of squawking infants and beaming mamas."

"Not tomorrow. There'll be other patients on medical, of course. But I'm going to concentrate. I've got a beautiful plan—all on paper. You know how it was in chem lab at high school—you put x and y into a test tube, held it over a Bunsen burner, and presto, you had something beautiful and new. Experiments with people are ten times as exciting. Whoa! You just passed the cottage where I live."

Nonchalantly, Nick backed up fifty yards. "I bet you're a crackerjack nurse, Kathy. But don't work too hard at it."

"I'll bet you'll be a crackerjack Ag Freshman." Kathy leaned over and gave her brother a hug. "And do work hard at it. That way it's more fun."

She watched him turn in the road, and winced at his shrieking tires. It made her happy to know that Nick had made up his mind to go to the Agricultural College. For a long time, he had insisted that he could learn on the ranch all he needed to know, that in spite of his father's wishes, he didn't need college training in agriculture.

Finally, Big Nick Martin had privately delved into books himself and plied his son with questions about soil chemistry and botany until young Nick announced firmly that he would have to go to ag school at Davis—whether his father wanted him to or not!

The light was on in the room she shared. Open suitcases and an array of fluffy clothes littered the beds; a golfbag was propped against the closet door. The pinks and reds and yellows and bright blues surprised Kathy. She was so used to seeing her roommate in uniform.

"No starch, no whites, nothing pinned on my head for two weeks!" Nadine Gregory folded a red chiffon dancing dress with tender loving care. "Vacation is the most beautiful word in the language."

"You're leaving in the morning?" Kathy yawned and kicked off her shoes.

"Praise heaven, yes. One more day of 202 would have finished me, I do believe."

"Is Collin worse?"

"Don't look at me as if I were responsible, Martin. I'm sorry for the boy, too. New X ray shows the femoral fracture has stopped knitting. And he's had an asthma attack. But there's still no earthly reason to be so difficult and downright rude!"

"You've got the cart before the horse, Greg," Kathy said earnestly. "Could be that emotional disturbance has changed his body chemistry and halted the healing of the bone. How would you feel if you'd caused the death of a famous artist—and your teacher?"

"Oh, Maxfield was more than that." Nadine was mildly interested. "Apparently the boy had moved in at the ranch. Like an apprentice in a Dickens novel. I still say it's no reason to throw books at the aides and spit out his food." She tucked in the last lacy blouse and snapped the suitcase shut. "All I hope for is a miracle: a nice quiet appendectomy in 202 when I get back from vacation."

A miracle. When Kathy stepped out of the house next morning, the sun was breaking through the early fog above the cliffs. It was a day for miracles, and in her apron pocket she had her plan for helping Collin, written out step by step.

The head nurse listened with surprising sympathy after they had gone over the charts.

"The staff considers 202 a room to avoid whenever possible," she said a little grimly. "It would certainly help if you could win the Monroe boy's confidence. But don't be disappointed if you are unable to produce results. At least you're nearer his age and, if I may say so, quite pretty." The older woman smiled a little wistfully, then, as if ashamed to be caught betraying any human emotion, pursed her lips and added crisply, "Please remember, Miss Martin, the patient in 202 is only one of eight. I don't encourage my nurses to play favorites."

Middle-aged caution was useful that first day. Collin was simply impossible—alternately full of complaints or listless and morosely silent.

Kathy was grateful when Steve called at suppertime. "Missed your day off," he said. "How's about a movie?

Or we could take in the Little Theatre in Monterey?"

"A movie would be lovely," Kathy sighed. "You can hold my hand while I sit in the dark and brood."

By the time Steve drove up, however, Kathy had cheered herself up with a swim in the ocean. She had put on her tawny yellow dress, a dark brown cardigan, and the agate earrings that had been Gail's present to her bridesmaids. The movie was unexpectedly amusing. The old-fashioned ice cream parlor with murals of Paris and Steve sitting across from her, open admiration in his eyes, put hospital problems right out of her mind.

Steve had run into Jenny and Sean in a pizza joint at San Tomás—The Henderson-Ramirez romance, he reported, seemed to be progressing nicely! Sean had a typical Linda story to report and made the most of it though he had never laid eyes on her. Linda, far away on an Austrian Alp, had no doubt spent hours composing a cablegram in rhyme to arrive at a strategic moment immediately after the wedding ceremony. The cable must have cost a fortune. The whole point depended on the timing, but it was delivered after everything was over and the guests had all departed. Linda had added the difference in time between Europe and California instead of subtracting, as anyone with half a mind would know you had to do!

The gay evening was almost over when Steve remembered one further bit of news.

"Sean says Matt's rise to fame via a by-line may be slightly delayed. Mr. and Mrs. Sherlock Holmes are not sure now that there has been dirty work at the cross-roads at all."

"You mean that there was nothing to this whole counterfeiting business, after all?" Kathy was properly outraged.

Steve nodded. "Seems an old Chinese importer gave the paper the tip that a fake painting had been foisted on the San Francisco Art Museum. Thousands of dollars were involved. Politics, too. But experts have been called in who say, 'Nuts to the guy from Chinatown.'"

"Oh, dear!" Kathy was disappointed. Gail and Matt could have explored the ghost towns after all.

But talking of painting gave Kathy an idea. Collin was an artist-in-training. Step one of her plan was to get the patient to express himself. Her book on psychotherapy had said that was the first thing to do.

"Psychotherapy? Long words like that leave me far behind," Steve teased.

"It means doing something to cure a heartache so the rest of the body can cure itself, as far as I could make out. My patient won't talk—maybe being an artist, he could get it out of his system by drawing pictures. Self-expression, they call it."

"Mmm," said Steve skeptically. "Finish your double banana split and I'll take you home."

IX

Trapped?

At seven-thirty the next morning, Kathy was seated behind the desk at the nurse's station in the medical-
surgical wing. Charts were in order, the two aides had
morning care under way, morning medications had been
prepared, and Kathy's jot sheet was tucked in the pocket
of her uniform. There was to be another series of blood
tests on Collin Monroe, and she was reaching for the
telephone to dial the laboratory when a man and a
woman stopped in front of the desk.

"Good morning!" The woman's voice was warm and
friendly, but Kathy could read the signs of strain in the
round, pretty face.

She glanced at the man. He was slightly built, his face
was weather-beaten and his hair was gray. But unmis-
takably he was Collin Monroe's father. Kathy would

have recognized anywhere the deep-set eyes, the sensitive, mobile mouth.

"You're here to see Collin, of course," she said warmly.

Mrs. Monroe looked pleased but puzzled. "That's right.
But I don't recall having seen you before."

"You haven't." Kathy smiled. "Collin looks very much
like his father. I was on night duty with him for a couple
of weeks."

Mr. Monroe peered over the counter at Kathy's name
tag. "Wait a minute. Aren't you the nurse who saved his
life after the accident? The one who stopped the bleeding?"

"But of course she is!" Mrs. Monroe held out both
hands. "We've wanted to say thanks—as if we could ever
tell you how . . ."

Kathy took the small hands in hers. "Don't think about
the accident," she said quickly. "I was there, that's all.
The problem now is to get Collin out of the doldrums
he's in. I've been wondering if he wouldn't enjoy having
a sketch pad and some pastels. He can use his hands and
arms freely, you know."

At noon, a package was delivered at the desk. Kathy
happened to meet an aide taking it down the hall.

"Is that for 202? I'll take it in."

"Thank you, Martin." The aide looked relieved. "I
probably shouldn't feel this way, but I'd just as soon
never go in there. That boy is the rudest patient I've
ever seen."

Kathy took the package without answering. She felt defensive about Collin, as if somehow she should explain away his behavior, but she couldn't spend her time apologizing for him. There were more constructive plans to be carried out.

"Your father thought you might enjoy having a sketch pad," she said, handing Collin the package. "We can put your table across the bed . . ."

She never had a chance to finish her sentence. With a burst of profanity, Collin picked up the package and hurled it across the room.

Kathy was furious. Without stopping to think about the nurse-patient relationship or anything else, she burst out with, "Now, you listen to me, young man. You've made every nurse and aide in this hospital want to stay out of this room. Suppose you stop behaving like a spoiled brat and show some manners!" She stopped short. This was no way to set up a relationship. She clamped her lips tight and walked across the room to pick up the package.

"Aw, cool it, Miss Martin. Don't be sore." Collin's voice was near the breaking point, but Kathy wasn't moved to sympathy. "It—it's just that this mess has got me drug down, way down," Collin went on. "Here I am like a five-year-old. Now I'm supposed to make pretty pictures with my crayons. . . ."

Kathy slowly took the wrappings off the package. She needed a few minutes to regain her composure.

"You can do as you please, Collin," she said coldly. "There are pastels here and a box of charcoal, if you haven't broken every piece. The paper is here. But nobody is asking you to use them."

She turned and walked out of the room. After all, as Mrs. Smith had pointed out, she had seven other patients to look after.

Kathy went through the rest of the day in a cloud of gloom. She went into Collin's room only when there was no one else she could send. It wasn't that she was still angry with Collin; she was angry with herself for having lost her temper and for having failed where she was sure she should have succeeded. By two-thirty she had such a splitting headache that she asked Mrs. Smith to take over for the last half-hour.

The older nurse looked at her quizzically. "202 been giving you a bad time today?"

Kathy's face flamed. "No worse than anyone else, I suppose."

She wasn't being wholly truthful, and she knew that Mrs. Smith knew it. Still, she couldn't bring herself to admit that she had failed in her project.

"Well, you go ahead, Martin. I'll take over. I assume your charts are complete?"

Kathy nodded and reached for her sweater. Outside the hospital the air was fresh, the ocean brilliant. She took a long, deep breath and decided to go for a walk on her way to the cottage. She wandered along a path that led through a grove of cypresses along the edge of the cliff above the ocean, her attention divided between the beauty of the landscape and a mental image of the scene in Collin's room. *Shall I try again or give up,* she was thinking, when a pair of legs startled her almost out of her wits. They were long legs encased in ladies' slacks, and when she first glimpsed them emerging from between two boulders, there was no sign of the rest of a body.

She peered around the huge rock and was astonished again. The legs belonged to the long, lean body of Old Mother Hubbard, who was down on her hands and knees peering intently at something.

"Miss Martin!" The older nurse seemed unabashed. "Too bad you are still wearing your uniform. I do believe I have found a fine sample of fossiliferous sandstone. Here, hold this magnifying glass for me a moment, will you?" She reached in a kit, came up with a sturdy hammer and proceeded to pound away at the boulder. As Kathy watched, wordless, she broke off a large chunk of rock. "Got you!" Miss Hubbard exclaimed. She backed out of the crevice and stood up. "Look here, this is really a treasure!" she said triumphantly.

Kathy couldn't see just why the piece of brownish-yellow rock should be considered a treasure, but she smiled weakly in response to Miss Hubbard's enthusiasm. "You're interested in geology?"

"I am chairman of the Ocean Cliff Rock Hounds," Miss Hubbard said with considerable pride. Then she looked more attentively at Kathy. "What is the matter with you, child? Did you forget to eat breakfast today? You youngsters, always inattentive to simple matters of health! No?

Fretting over your patients, perhaps? Somebody on the critical list?"

"A patient, yes. Not a D.I., not dangerously ill yet. At least I don't think so."

Stumbling a little in her eagerness, Kathy outlined Collin's problems and her vain attempt to get through to him. "Everyone agrees what's wrong—we want to get him to talk about the dead man. This book I read said the indirect method of self-revelation was often therapeutic in cases of emotional disturbance. It said 'approach each individual through his established cultural pattern.'"

"Hmph!" Miss Hubbard interrupted. "You have to crack a lot of words to get at a plain, common-sense idea! You say the boy was studying art? Why don't you give him some paper and pencils and let him fiddle?"

Kathy brightened. "That's just what I did, Miss Hubbard. I asked his parents to send a sketch pad and pastels and I took them in to him and adjusted his bed and he threw the pad across the room."

"Give your patient time, Miss Martin. That's what the books always leave out—the minutes and hours and days. Try a little patience, Miss Martin."

Kathy did not have to wait long. The sketch pad was on the bedside table next morning. Collin was asleep. She bent down and examined the soft colored chalks. They showed signs of having been used. Quietly, so as not to disturb the patient, she took the pad over to the window. On the first page was a rough sketch of sea and rocks in muted colors. It had good composition, but was nothing remarkable—no more than any person with a talent for drawing would see with an outward eye. She was about to replace the sketch pad when the corner of a page slid forward. The sheet had been torn out, crumpled and then laid back in the tablet.

A lone Monterey cypress growing out of jagged rocks stared out at her. Somehow the tree seemed, before her eyes, to develop gnarled, humanlike fingers grasping at the surrounding rocks. And the rocks were undoubtedly in the rough form of a human figure.

Surely, Kathy thought, this is an expression of someone who feels trapped. Collin, trapped by the guilty feelings related to the accident? Somehow Kathy began to doubt it. True, Maxfield's car had crashed against a boulder jutting out in the road, but the stones in the drawing were not the attackers. They were strangled in the grasp of the cypress tree. And there were no cypresses on the Santa Cruz highway. The emotion that had found expression here did not seem connected with the accident. Yet, the emotion itself was strong and revealing. It meant something to Collin or he would not have crumpled and, afterward, hidden the sheet of paper.

With a glance at the patient to be sure that he was still asleep, Kathy slipped the drawing in her pocket and went to the desk at the nurse's station to show it to the head nurse. Mrs. Smith held the drawing this way and that while Kathy talked. Then she handed it back with a shake of her head.

"I don't see all that you read into it. The picture looks like all those framed things in the shops at Carmel, but then I'm not up on art. One witch tree post card looks to me like another. I could be wrong, though," she added. "Why don't you give it to the Monroe boy's doctor, Miss Martin? His office is across the street from the Red Cross building where you'll have your class this afternoon."

"Could I do that?" Kathy asked eagerly. "You see, if Collin . . ."

The head nurse cut her off. "The light is on for Room 107, Miss Martin. It has been on quite a while."

There was a note of accusation in Miss Smith's voice that sent Kathy down the hall at a swift pace. She'd been reprimanded before for playing favorites among her patients. It was hard not to, when you had such a challenging problem as Collin's.

There wasn't much time to mull over the picture in the morning, but a glance at it during her coffee break confirmed Kathy's opinion that it held at least a clue that might lead to the boy's recovery. *The witch tree,* Mrs. Smith had called it. But the witch tree of post card fame had no green branches. Still, now that Mrs. Smith had mentioned it, Kathy could see a resemblance.

"It's not much like the real tree Steve and I picnic under," she said to herself, "but with all the meaning changed it's a good deal like the painting I liked so much that day in San Francisco."

She would write to Kelley and ask her to find out the artist's name on the painting in Mr. Amos X. Gray's shop.

X

The Lonely Abalone

"Do you have an appointment, Miss Martin?" The doctor's waiting room in Monterey was crowded with patients: young mothers in Bermuda shorts, a haggard look on their faces and squirming babies in their arms, a stout man balancing a crutch against a rubber plant, a wispy old lady with hair that was an amazing pink in the late afternoon sunlight, two large-bosomed females who stopped their discussion of last night's T.V. program to glare at Kathy as she breezed confidently up to the receptionist's window and gave her name.

Kathy was still in uniform. She hadn't much time. The Red Cross clinic opened at six.

"I just wanted to see Dr. McLean a moment. It's not for myself. For one of his patients."

The words fell on deaf ears. The receptionist might

as well have been a phonograph record intoning "You'll have to make an appointment." She leafed through a calendar without a glance at Kathy's pleading eyes. "Say, a week from Thursday, Miss Martin?"

"Look, I'm on day duty at Ocean Cliff."

"If a morning appointment is inconvenient, Doctor can see you after four on October 1st."

"This year or next?"

Kathy knew her exasperation was unreasonable. All those people in the waiting room needed Dr. McLean, too. But she had rehearsed what she wanted to say so carefully, all the way up on the bus, only to be balked by this little snip of a receptionist who didn't even have sense enough to look up from her calendar when she was talking to people.

Frustration hurried her footsteps, and she scarcely noticed where she was going until she found herself at Fisherman's Wharf. Monterey Harbor at sunset is not a place to nurse disappointment. The rocky coast swung in a smooth curve around the bay, where dozens of fishing smacks and pleasure boats bobbed up and down in the water. Circling gulls and cormorants, wings rosy with reflected light, added their cries to the delighted squeals of children who raced on the small beach, challenging the incoming tide with pretended terror.

Kathy walked out to the end of the pier and leaned on the railing. She watched two little dark-skinned girls in abbreviated bathing suits drag rough lengths of seaweed from the water to use for jump-ropes. Beyond, a group of half-grown boys were leaping from their boat and swimming for shore with strong, easy strokes. The sea, the sky, the beach—all nature was friendly to youth.

Kathy's hand went unconsciously to the crumpled drawing in her pocket. "Just a few weeks ago," she said to herself, "Collin Monroe might have been one of those swimmers. And then—a twist of a steering wheel on the highway, a sense of guilt, and his body refuses to heal . . . But it *can* heal—given half a chance. I'll waylay that doctor in the hospital tomorrow."

Kathy turned away from the gay scene reluctantly. Her Red Cross course would begin in less than an hour. She looked around for a place to get supper. Low buildings lined the pier on one side. Eating places, fish markets, souvenir and shell shops elbowed one another in gay parade. Toward the end of the pier, on the side near the open sea, she came upon a little hole-in-the-wall restaurant entrancingly called *The Lonely Abalone*.

"Really too much," she muttered to herself, and walked into the restaurant.

The coloring of the one small room was an opaque version of an abalone shell—gray and a range of off-white from mother-of-pearl to almost pink. On the ocean side a huge single-paned, oval window framed the sea. Around the walls were shelves of knickknacks—figurines, shells, pottery and glass and china. They were casually arranged, and there was enough wall space to avoid a crowded, too-busy appearance. Nor was there a crowded look to the tables along the window and in the middle of the room. In fact, except for a young couple holding hands and admiring each other instead of the scenery, Kathy was alone in the room. Of course, it was late for lunch and early for dinner.

She sat down and studied the typewritten menu. Seafood—nothing else would be appropriate here. Gail wouldn't hesitate—she always took Crab Louis. And Linda would take the abalone because abalone was such a romantic-sounding word. But Kathy didn't like abalone.

The important question of what to order was still undecided when the waitress came to her table.

"I think—the shrimp salad, please. No, make it the swordfish—and coffee," she added hurriedly.

"Aren't you Miss Martin? From the hospital?"

Kathy looked up in surprise and held out her hand. "Mrs. Monroe! I didn't realize this was your place. I thought you had a gift shop and Mr. Monroe took out fishing trips."

"We have and he does," the plump little woman laughed pleasantly. "Pictures, vases, all those little animals, everything in here is for sale. Folks on the wharf generally serve food as well. Lunch and short orders mostly. It helps pay the rent but keeps both of us busy. That's why we had to move Collin down from Santa Cruz, you know." Tears came to her eyes. "You know how it is with an only child. At least, you don't know, do you?" she added nervously. "I'd better go broil your fish. I'd like to talk to you a few minutes, then, if you don't mind."

A couple of other customers came in, and Mrs. Monroe had no time for conversation when she brought Kathy's plate. There was a lull when she brought the coffee and Kathy impulsively said, "You must have missed your son this summer. I understand he was living at Mr. Maxfield's home."

"We did. Though it's always a problem in the summer, with school out and my being away all day. And it was too good an opportunity to miss. Mr. Maxfield invited Collin because he thought our son had talent. His sister usually kept house for him. She's gone to Italy for a year." Mrs. Monroe seemed only too glad to talk. "Mr. Maxfield was a wonderful man. He gave his sister the money for the trip and insisted that she go."

"Have you heard from her, Mrs. Monroe, since her brother's death?" A thought flashed into Kathy's mind. It could be that this sister blamed Collin. That would explain his emotional upset.

The mother flushed red. "I—I don't know, Miss Martin," she answered hesitantly. "A letter came several days ago. Air mail, with an Italian stamp. I can't face watching Collin read it. The poor boy blames himself enough, already, though the doctor seems satisfied that after the first shock he has come through as well as can be expected."

"Maybe he is worrying because of the sister's reaction," Kathy said quietly.

"That could be!" Mrs. Monroe hurried away and into a back room. In a moment she thrust a thin blue envelope

into Kathy's hand. "You're a nurse, Miss Martin. You could choose a good time to give our boy the letter—or whether to give it to him at all."

"But oughtn't you to open and read it first, Mrs. Monroe?"

"Oh, I couldn't. It's addressed to Collin. They are his friends, not mine. If you don't mind, I'd like to leave the whole thing in your hands."

All through the Red Cross lecture on blood transfusion and the demonstration that followed, Kathy's thoughts kept slipping away to her patient in Room 202. The letter from Miss Maxfield might give just the opening she'd been waiting for. She could watch his reactions when he read it and get him to talk.

When she undressed that night she took the letter and Collin's picture from her pocket. She stuck the picture in the mirror to study it.

"There's a clue in that drawing," she said to herself. "If only I could read it correctly!"

XI

Oxygen Tent

Collin's chart showed no change when Kathy came on duty next morning. An aide took him his breakfast. Kathy passed her in the hall fifteen minutes later taking the tray back to the kitchen, scarcely touched.

"Bones won't knit on a sip of juice, I told 202. But he just clamped his teeth shut. Stubborn!"

Kathy didn't answer. She was busy preparing old Mrs. Talbot in 106 for surgery. The surgeon and anesthetist had already arrived, and the surgical nurse had asked Kathy to assist at the operation. That's the way a small, country hospital managed—one surgical nurse on call and someone on the staff to act as circulating nurse. There was not, as a rule, more than one surgical case a week.

"And Kelley thought I wouldn't get experience here. She was really way off," Kathy said to herself as she exchanged her striped cap for the turban worn in the operating room.

The patient was already draped. The anesthetist, with his tanks and tubes and measuring instruments, stood ready at the head of the table. A tank of oxygen and a jar of plasma hanging from a standard was nearby. Kathy would administer these if needed. She would also run any errands, the only person allowed to go in and out of the room during the operation. Now, as circulating nurse, she waited just outside the door to help the "scrub" nurse and the surgeon on with their sterile gloves. The routine of surgery was thoroughly familiar to her, but the drama always cast its spell.

The patient was on the operating table about an hour. The surgical nurse went with her to the small recovery room. The surgeon and anesthetist disappeared, leaving Kathy and an aide to sterilize the instruments and clean up. It was eleven o'clock before she had time to look in on Collin. He had his little transistor radio going and seemed unusually cheerful.

"Dig this horn," he said when Kathy walked in. "That cat is really too much."

It seemed a good time to produce the letter from Italy.

"Some mail for you," Kathy said as casually as she could, and laid the letter within reach of his hand. Then she busied herself moving pieces on the dresser.

In the mirror she could see Collin examine the envelope. He hesitated, turned pale. Suddenly Kathy wished she had the letter back again. Perhaps she ought to have consulted Mrs. Smith or the doctor. This wasn't a routine "get-well" card.

The voice of a girl singing a blues song came over the radio. The single sheet of paper was out of the envelope now. Over the sound of the radio, Kathy could hear the sudden change in Collin's breathing—the heavy sound of asthmatic wheezing. She whirled around as the letter dropped from his hand.

The attack was a bad one. It was obvious that he was going to need a shot. Epinephrine was the drug called for by the doctor's standing orders. Kathy moved swiftly, hurrying to the supply room off the nurse's station.

She worked swiftly, measuring, double-checking her measurements, preparing the hypodermic syringe. By the time she strode back into Room 202, Collin was gasping for breath. Quickly she injected the medicine, and waited. It seemed to have no effect. The gasping was getting more and more labored. And then she saw the danger signal—blue lips.

The shadow of someone passing the door caught her eye. "Mrs. Smith!" she cried in sudden panic. Collin's heart was racing. Kathy didn't even have to lean down to hear the gurgling sound in his chest. "Mrs. Smith!" she called again.

The head nurse came into the room and took one look at the patient. "Oxygen, Martin! Bring the tank over, please."

Events moved swiftly. The mask was fitted over Collin's face, the tubes inserted into his nostrils.

"Call Dr. McLean, will you?" Mrs. Smith was counting Collin's pulse. "Then come back in and stay with him. I've got a D.I. down the hall."

Kathy moved like a puppet on a string, down the hall, to the telephone, and back again to the room. She could see that Collin was better. A little less cyanotic, the gasps less desperate. The life-saving oxygen was doing its work.

"Dr. McLean is in surgery," Kathy said. Her voice was shaking, but she couldn't help it. "He'll be up in about twenty minutes. Do you want someone else?"

"I think that won't be necessary. Just keep the oxygen going. You've given epinephrine?"

"One dose," Kathy answered.

"Let's try another."

By the time Dr. McLean arrived, Mrs. Smith had left the room. Collin was more comfortable, though still fighting for breath. The doctor ordered an oxygen tent.

"You'll be more comfortable that way," he said to Collin. "You're all right now, boy."

An asthma patient needed plenty of reassurance; there are few things as terrifying as the feeling of having your breath cut off, of being unable to take in air.

Kathy was adjusting the oxygen tent when she noticed the letter. It had slipped to the floor, half-hidden under the bed. She reached down and tucked it in her pocket. Her own heart was racing; she knew she should tell Dr. McLean about the moments before this attack.

"You seem to have things well in hand," the doctor went on in a low voice, standing near the door of 202.

"Give him an I.V. injection if necessary. And call me if there are any indications of cyanosis again. I don't like these attacks he's been having. We'll have to do another chest X ray. I still have the feeling that there may have been some bronchial injury that we haven't located."

Kathy took a deep breath. She had to tell the doctor, but it wasn't easy to begin. *Mrs. Monroe asked me to give him the letter,* she argued with herself. *And there were no orders forbidding him to get mail.* The excuses were not valid, and she couldn't even fool herself. She had been overeager, impetuous and stubborn—determined to cure the patient by some miracle. A nurse's job is to carry out orders to the best of her ability, not to act on her own. Trying to help Collin, she had hurt him. Yet, if she told the doctor, it might mean her dismissal!

You will make mistakes. To fail to report a mistake . . . cannot be condoned or forgiven. Miss Wilson's words, from her very first lecture in Nursing Ethics. They were a part of Kathy's training, and she responded to them.

"If he's well enough tomorrow, we'll go ahead and take him to X ray," the doctor was saying.

"Dr. McLean." Kathy's knees were trembling, but she knew what she had to do. A little breathlessly she explained about the letter.

"You gave the patient a letter from the dead man's sister?" Dr. McLean's round face flushed with anger. "What did it say to bring on this attack?"

Kathy held the thin blue sheet out to him without speaking. She was close to tears.

The doctor fumbled for his glasses and scanned the closely written sheet, reading snatches aloud.

For the first few days I couldn't bring myself to write coherently even to you who were so close to my dear brother. . . . You must not feel a burden of responsibility for the accident. It is for us who loved him to keep alive the memory of a noble life. . . . You and I know that Edwin Maxfield was a saint.

McLean took off his glasses and wiped a sentimental tear from his eye. His exasperation had melted completely.

"A message like this from Miss Maxfield should be a comfort to the boy. You were right to give it to him, Miss Martin . . . though perhaps consultation between physician and nurse would be advisable in the future—"

Kathy was so surprised at the contents of the letter, so relieved at Dr. McLean's change of heart, that she forgot to mention that she *had* tried to consult him. She just stood and beamed as he hurried out of the door.

Collin was under sedation and slept most of the afternoon. Kathy was in and out of his room several times, but had no opportunity to return the letter until just before three.

Collin's light went on while she was making up her charts. He wanted the curtains closed. The sun was in his eyes. Kathy put Miss Maxfield's letter on the night table.

"It's a beautiful letter, Collin. I—read it. You see now, don't you, that no one blames you—for what happened?"

Collin shrugged his shoulders impatiently. "Who said they did? I told Max three days before we smashed that the steering rod was far gone."

Deliberately he closed his eyes. It was a gesture of dismissal.

XII

Of Elephants and Snails

Kathy stared out of the car window as if the dark landscape held a clue to Collin Monroe's problems. She was on her way back to the seaside cottage after a long evening at her Red Cross course. The physician who had conducted the class—a woman—lived farther down the coast at Big Sur and had invited Kathy to ride with her.

After a few moments of talk about Kathy's Alaskan project, conversation had languished. The steady whirr of the wheels on the highway lulled Kathy to drowsiness. Flashes of the busy day came to her mind—the frightening sound of Collin's heavy breathing, the swift, precise gestures of the head nurse as she stood above the boy placing the oxygen mask, the warmth of Miss Maxfield's letter—but, most of all, Collin's surprise that anyone should think he was to blame for the accident.

Still, the letter had disturbed him greatly. Why?

The car swerved to the right to let a bus go by, and Kathy became conscious of her surroundings.

"The nurses' cottage is just around the bend," Kathy said. "I'm afraid I haven't been very good company."

The older woman smiled, "Neither have I. I had a patient on my mind."

"So doctors worry, too!" Kathy laughed with slight embarrassment. "Sometimes we nurses think we're the only ones! Thanks for the ride, Dr. Perez."

She watched the car gather speed as it started down the highway, and stood for a moment, sniffing the salt air and admiring the dark pattern of the cypresses over the water. Then, whistling in her usual monotone, she started down the long path to the cottage.

She heard a noise and stopped whistling to listen. Footsteps—and not far behind! She quickened her pace, and the footsteps changed to a run. Kathy ran, too, more and more alarmed. She had almost reached the door when she heard her name called.

"Martin! I'm home!" The voice was Linda Garfield's! Linda, who wasn't supposed to arrive from Europe for another month.

Linda's arms were loaded with packages. They scattered like autumn leaves when the two girls embraced.

"If it weren't for all those post cards you sent of cathedrals and museums, I'd think you spent your summer buying presents," Kathy said, when they had piled the packages and themselves on the bed.

Linda kicked off her shoes and snuggled her head in the pillows.

"I got homesick. The family is coming by ship, but I figured if I flew I could surprise Jim on his birthday. And then we came down to Appleton to stay with his folks. You weren't at the ranch and I couldn't wait another minute to see you—so I hopped a bus. At the hospital they said you weren't on PM any more. And then you got out of that car and I thought I'd never catch you on the path. I always said your legs were too long!"

"Did you have a good time in Europe?" Kathy asked.

"Super! We ate snails in Paris and I almost couldn't, remembering your mother's battle with the creatures in her garden. And when we hit Germany my father bought a Volkswagen. Blue and very cute. He's going to give it to me when they get it home—if they do. Jim says it might have a chance of surviving now that I'm no longer the driver."

"Pay Doctor-to-be Telford no mind," Kathy said. "You drive perfectly well even if Jim never lets you take the wheel."

A faraway look came into Linda's blue eyes, and the shadow of a smile played around her lips. "Maybe I shouldn't have written Jim about having to borrow a bridge."

"Golden Gate or San Rafael?"

Linda was perfectly serious. "It was the first day I drove, and it was just a little bridge. You don't know how fascinating it is to go down lanes that could lead anywhere. Castles, or ruined monasteries, or tiny thatched-roof farm houses where they sell honey dipped from a wicker basket. Only this lane led to a dead end with ditches on both sides—and even with a Volkswagen, I ended up with the back wheels in a ditch. About a half-mile up the road I found a bridge over the ditch—and the boards were loose, so we carried them one at a time —Mom and I—you know Dad's got a bad back. We didn't let him lift. Anyhow, we got the bridge under our wheels. Then we drove out in style. We carried the boards back on the roof of the car and rebuilt the farmer's bridge. That was before we got the dent in the top, of course," she added pensively.

"What kind of dent? Your car didn't turn over?" Kathy had grown accident-conscious. There was anxiety in her voice.

Linda shook her head. "An elephant sat on it."

"Hey, Garfield, that's too much, really too much."

Linda giggled. "That's what the policeman said, except he was talking German and he said it in ten-syllable words. He wasn't a German cop—one of those plump Swiss *gendarmes* with white gloves and a whistle as big as a clarinet. But it was the elephant-trainer who looked like Jim who really made me homesick."

"I don't dig you, Garfield. Are you sure you feel all right? No dizziness? No spots before your eyes?"

Linda giggled again. "We were at Zurich in Switzerland. On our way to dinner at one of those restaurants perched on the side of an Alp, I heard circus music and naturally pulled up at the curb to see the parade go by. Clowns, ladies in spangles on horseback, a simply darling tiger in a gilded cage. And then the elephants—six of them waltzing to the music of a calliope. And there was this trainer that looked like Jim, in a red fez waving a long stick with a tassle on the end."

"And that made you homesick?"

Linda ignored the interruption. "All at once, one of the elephants turned and began climbing on the Volkswagen's roof."

"Heavens above!"

"He was very deliberate, very careful. Mom screamed, of course, and quite a crowd gathered. The trainer ran back. He felt terrible. He got the elephant to climb down. Just by a word, spoken in French. Mom understands French, and she stopped screaming when he explained that his elephant was trained to go to a blue stool in the ring—so, the Volkswagen being blue . . . There wasn't any real damage, just this—this elephant-sized dent in the roof. The parade went on, and then we drove away."

"Where did the policeman come in?" Kathy asked patiently. Getting a story out of Linda was like climbing a spiral stairway. You went around and around until you came to the top.

"I drove on to the village where the restaurant is. The *gendarme* ran out and stopped us. He pointed to the roof of the car—seemed to think we had an accident. I guess he wanted to be helpful. We couldn't understand very well. I never will understand any German. I ex-

plained with gestures about the elephant. I did everything but waltz up on that roof myself. But he got more
and more suspicious. Had we reported the accident?
How many *tot?* That means killed. Anyhow, he ended up
taking us to a cute little jail and wouldn't let us go until
he'd located the circus. And the elephant trainer came
on a motorcycle to get us out. That was when I noticed
how his eyes were exactly like Jim's—you know, kind of
deep set and dreamy. And so I decided to come home.
And Gail and Matt met my plane and we had a divine
birthday party for Jim and they want us all to come up
to the city tomorrow because Steve said that's your day
off. That's what I really came down tonight ahead of
time to tell you."

XIII

Mr. and Mrs. Sherlock at Home

"Ask *Mrs.* Sherlock anything you want to know about Chinese scrolls," Matt said, as he came in from the kitchenette balancing seven steaming mugs on a tray. Gail hurriedly moved pieces on the coffee table and watched her husband set down the tray with as much pride as if he had accomplished a feat of surpassing valor.

"The perfect host," Kelley murmured, looking up from her place on the window seat.

Lunch was almost over, and she was occupying the pauses between courses by making thumbnail sketches of the roof tops and harbor. Gail and Matt had chosen the fourth-floor walk-up apartment because of the view. They knew just the way the old room should be furnished. At the moment, however, the furnishings consist-

ed of the built-in window seat, two tired chairs left behind by former tenants, the fruitwood coffee table that
had been the bridesmaids' present, a grandfather clock
Matt had inherited from his New England ancestors, and
a large supply of orange crates.

One of the chairs was occupied by Merry, the Dalmatian puppy. The other was piled high with books.
Gail, Kathy, Linda and Jim sat on the floor. Steve wandered around the room, thinking up new questions to
ask about Matt's unwritten scoop.

They had talked of little else since they'd met Gail
outside the museum that morning. She had led the way
to the Recent Accessions Room, where the subject of all
the controversy was on exhibition. A wealthy old lady,
she explained, had left the museum quite a large sum in
her will, and the objects purchased for the museum were
on view for the first time. There were a hand mirror and
a pottery cat from an Egyptian tomb, the head of a
Roman emperor minus the tip of his nose and a Russian
ikon. The most valuable of all was a long, narrow paper
scroll covered with Chinese writing and embellished
with birds and beasts and a glimpse of a snow-capped
mountain. Chon Fang. Ninth Century.

Steve didn't know much about art. He wasn't im-
pressed, as Kathy was, with the beauty of the little landscape down in one corner, or with the delicate shading
of grays and blacks that Gail pointed out. He couldn't
whip up any excitement over the fact that the scroll was
supposed to be one of the earliest examples of Chinese

—or any other—painting in any American museum. But the mystery of whether the thing was authentic or a fraud held his attention.

Was the scroll a modern imitation, as Ho Wong, the herbalist from Chinatown, insisted? If so, the reputations of two important art critics would drop down a well, to say nothing of the popularity of the curator of the museum. And the public would have been cheated out of $10,000 of the old lady's bequest.

Matt, Gail said, was thoroughly convinced that a forgery had been committed. Proving it, however, was tricky, and his paper could not afford to print the story without absolute proof.

"If a ninth-century artist didn't do the painting, who did?" Linda asked.

Gail sighed. "That's what we'd like to know. There are three thousand artists in San Francisco alone and as many again in Hong Kong. The scroll was supposed to have been smuggled in from there."

"Then there's the Left Bank in Paris," Linda said, warming to the subject.

Jim snorted. "According to you, they're all busy eating snails."

After the stop at the museum the group had moved on to Matt and Gail's apartment. Matt, who worked at night, was up and waiting for them and had started frying the chicken. Lunch was ready when Kelley strolled in. She was in uniform, prepared to go on duty directly after the luncheon.

All through the meal Matt had answered Steve's searching questions about the case. The art critic on the paper didn't go along with the theory that the scroll was a fake, Matt explained.

"That's why I got a shot at the story," he added with a grin. "None of the experts will come out and say the thing isn't authentic. And the art dealer from whom the painting was bought—a reputable and knowledgeable man—was outraged that anyone should dare to question it."

"Where did the dealer get the scroll?" Steve asked.

The puzzle was like one of those chess games that went on interminably at the firehouse between alarms.

"Apparently it came into his hands after World War II. I had a devil of a time getting any information out of him at first. He said he had to protect the name of the person who smuggled it in. Then suddenly, a couple of days later, he mailed me the name on the back of one of his cards. A Merchant Marine captain who made the run between San Francisco and Hong Kong."

"Have you traced the smuggler?"

Matt nodded his head. "That wasn't hard, worse luck. The morgue at the paper produced a clipping from the files in ten minutes: the notice of his death in a lumber camp in Oregon. About a week ago. Pictures and everything . . . *Ex-War Hero Meets Death from Falling Limb after Braving Enemy Waters During War.* Et cetera."

"Which left Matt nowhere," Gail said, carefully dividing an apple pie into seven wedges. "We thought we'd have to give up. A Los Angeles art expert saved our lives . . . at least temporarily. He didn't exactly agree with Mr. Ho that the paper was wrong and the ink made with modern glue. What he did was to point out that critics had been consulted by the museum curator *before* the purchase, so that any opinion they now gave could hardly be called unprejudiced."

"Your herbalist bases his claim on the paper?"

"Just the *feel* of it. It can't be analyzed chemically, of course, without ruining the picture. And you can't do that to a painting that may be two thousand years old."

"What's so special about Chinese paper, anyway?" Jim wanted to know.

"That's what I wondered," Gail said. "Until I began looking it up in the library. Who would have thought the Chinese were drawing lovely pictures on paper way back in the second century B.C., when our ancestors were still scratching on stone? They made the paper out of linen, then rice, on a hand press—and it had a special glaze that made it last—but not forever, of course. That's why a really old painting on paper is a rare find. This one is supposed to be by the artist Chon Fang. There's just one other in the country—in New York." With enthusiasm Gail leafed through one of the books. "If Merry hasn't eaten it for breakfast, I can show you the history of Chinese paintings in all the different dynasties—on a chart—like the bones of a body."

At this point, Matt went out to get refills of coffee and returned to brag about his wife's thorough research.

Steve nursed his coffee cup. "We know Gail's like a bulldog when she gets an idea between her teeth," he laughed. "It does look as if paper is the crux of your mystery, Matt. Wouldn't it be a good idea to get a paper expert from somewhere to give his opinion?"

Matt nodded and pulled out a letter from New York. "That's just what I have done. The man is on his way to San Francisco."

XIV

Private-Duty Nurse

At the hospital next morning, Kathy found the head nurse studying the charts with a frown on her face.

"Is anything wrong?" Kathy asked.

She was feeling especially cheerful. The day in San Francisco and the ride down the coast with Steve had been perfect. And this morning the sun had come over the mountain just in time to make a path of sparkling color from the cottage to the hospital door. Real California weather—and Californians saw so little of it.

"Nothing serious," the nurse answered. "The patient in 202—"

"Did he have the chest X ray?" Kathy interrupted anxiously.

"Yes. Negative for any signs of injury. There's still a lot of congestion, of course. He's under moist oxygen part of the day. But he had such a restless night and made so many demands that the staff couldn't cope with them. Dr. McLean has requested a Special for graveyard duty. He thinks you're the best nurse to put on the job."

"Does he, really?" Kathy flushed with pleasure. "I've never done any private-duty nursing," she added.

"It will leave me short-handed again," the head nurse sighed. "But if you want that job you'd better go back and get some sleep."

"Let me help first with breakfasts," Kathy offered. "Then I'll take a swim and rest until time for my class in Monterey. I'll come directly from the Red Cross to night duty."

"Skip Monterey," the older woman advised. "I'll phone and explain about the shift in schedule. I don't envy you having eight hours with the Monroe boy. He's a pest."

Kathy spent an hour on the beach. She didn't feel sleepy in the least but obediently went back to bed. She thought about Alaska and wondered if the orders would ever come. Kelley hadn't even mentioned it yesterday. She thought about Collin, the way he was, and the experiences from which he had learned to be that way. It was ridiculous to expect him to sleep through the night when obviously he had something nagging at his mind.

Drowsily, she thought up ways to amuse him. She'd tell him about Gail and Matt's apartment overhanging Fisherman's Wharf, and about the great mystery of the counterfeit scroll. Make him think about something outside himself—everybody likes to play who-done-it—and an artist ought to know about Chinese painting—all those lovely names of brush strokes in Gail's book.

She thought about Steve. He had kissed her last night at the cottage door. And they hadn't had a fight for ages. And he'd asked her to go dancing next week . . . could she wear her bridesmaid's dress? Or just a sweater and skirt with his pin on the pocket?

Kathy fell asleep and dreamed that she was dressed in a Chinese costume dancing with a Roman Emperor with a broken nose. It felt strange to get up in the dark of night and put on a uniform to go on duty. Strange to eat a can of beef stew and cheese cake for "breakfast." She washed up the dishes in the little kitchenette and looked at her watch. Just nine o'clock and she wasn't due at the hospital until eleven.

"If Collin is restless, he'll like company earlier," she said to herself, and walked over to the hospital. *A private duty nurse.*

Mrs. Smith was sitting at the desk and did not look up until Kathy spoke. "Oh, it's you, Martin." She held out Collin's chart. "I hope you don't have too bad a night. He's under sedation now. You can repeat the dosage at your discretion. The doctor has increased his calcium. And you are to put him under oxygen if his breathing goes bad. He had an X ray today. No progress on the leg. A young boy like that—his bones ought to knit in no time!"

"But he's not just any boy," Kathy said to herself. "He's Collin Monroe who was driving a car when his friend was killed. That hangs over his head like a sword of Damocles . . . or maybe it doesn't."

With a start she remembered the day he read Miss Maxfield's letter. Maybe something else was making him afraid to get well. But it was going to take more than calcium and oxygen to make the cells that repair bones begin to function.

She took the chart, checked her watch with the clock on the wall and with a smile of anticipation opened the door of 202. The room was dark, her patient asleep, wheezing slightly but requiring no immediate attention. Across from the bed, near the window, Kathy adjusted a small night light. She pulled up a comfortable chair as she had seen other private nurses do, and sat down to study her chart. It was nice having just one patient. You could give him all your attention without feeling hurried.

It didn't take long to memorize the familiar chart. She listened for a while to the beat of the ocean waves, tried to think up words to describe the sound of an incoming tide. Then she glanced through some of Collin's unread magazines. An hour went by, and Kathy was beginning to be bored with private-duty nursing. She was really glad when Collin woke.

He didn't ask for anything, didn't speak at all. But Kathy knew that he was awake by his changed breathing, and she could feel that he was staring at her with eyes too bright and feverish.

"You're looking sharp, man. Fine as wine." She hoped he was glad to find her there.

The boy closed his eyes and mumbled something Kathy could not hear. She came and stood by the bed. "I didn't hear you," she said lightly.

"Forget the jive, I told you. That talk is for artists. Who wants to be an artist?"

"You mustn't grieve so, Collin, for Mr. Maxfield. You're going to be an artist and as good a one as he was."

"And a saint, too, I suppose . . . 'You and I know he was a saint,'" the boy quoted. His voice was indistinct. The effect of the sleeping pill had not entirely worn off.

Kathy saw that her patient was drowsy. By the time she had shifted his position a little and smoothed the pillows, he was off again to a restless sleep.

It was almost dawn before Collin stirred again. When he woke, he seemed much calmer, rested and ready to be amused. Kathy brought him a cup of warm milk and the medication indicated on the chart. While he sipped the milk, she chatted about her day off in San Francisco. One of the tasks of a nurse is to bring a little of the outside world into the sickroom to divert attention from the patient's discomfort or pain. The luncheon in the half-furnished apartment, the puppy named— or misnamed— for Perry Mason, Linda's tale of her encounter with the elephant in Europe all made amusing anecdotes. It was a pleasure to hear Collin's mild chuckles.

The stars were still visible, but the sky was a pale luminous gray.

"Another day without fog!" Kathy said, drawing open the curtains.

She took her place in the easy chair once more, but continued the casual conversation. Time enough later, she thought, for further sedation.

"Do you know anything about Chinese scrolls?" she asked.

A pistol shot could not have been more devastating than Collin's reaction. He wheezed, tried to speak, and then broke into hysterical weeping.

Kathy was frightened. Had she done the wrong thing *again?* Anxiously she took his pulse. It was strong but very irregular. She reached for the button to signal for help.

Collin caught her hand abruptly and gasped in a hoarse whisper, "How much do you know?"

"What do you mean?"

"Are you in with the cops? Are they on to the forgery?"

The boy's skin was gray-white. Swiftly Kathy prepared a hypo, wondering whether she ought to call the doctor. But all the while she was performing the duties of a nurse her mind was racing ahead. Had she stumbled on the secret of Collin's emotional distress? She had grown so fond of the boy, believed in him. Was he just a fraud, with only the fear of being caught?

The hypo was having its effect. He was calmer now. The color was coming back into his face. The danger of collapse was over. She started to move away from the bed but he held on to her skirt.

"Is there something you want to talk about?" she asked in her most professional manner.

Collin shook his head violently. "I can't tell anybody."

"You can talk to me," Kathy said. "A nurse is different from other people. Do you know about the Florence Nightingale Oath? I couldn't tell if I wanted to."

Collin clamped his lips tight shut. A long sigh shook his whole frame. After a minute there was another of those deep gasps, and then a slight wheeze.

Kathy went out to the desk and requested a tank of oxygen.

"Another asthma attack?" the night nurse asked.

"The beginning of one. I think we can stave it off with the oxygen. The patient has had sedation. I want him to get some sleep."

Kathy was trembling when she finally sat down again in the chair by the window. "*So that's the trap he's in,*" she thought, remembering the sketch sticking in her mirror. "No wonder Collin's fractured leg won't heal. As long as he lies here, helpless, he won't have to take the responsibility for what he's done. And I'm in that trap with him. Matt's story has fallen right in my lap and I can't even hint at the truth. It's Collin Monroe's secret and Collin, no matter what else he is, is my patient."

With her inner ear she could hear the dry voice of Miss Wilson, the nursing school director, speaking the words of the Florence Nightingale Oath: *I will hold in confidence all personal matters committed to my keeping, and all family affairs coming to my knowledge in the practice of my calling.* That would be her duty even if a patient confessed to a crime far worse than forgery.

XV

Steve Kovak Prescribes

On his way from a Forest Ranger station next afternoon, Steve stopped at the nurses' cottage to pick up Kathy for an early picnic supper before her class in Monterey.

"Where do we eat?" he said as she settled herself in the car. "Under the witch tree, as usual?"

"Oh, no!" Kathy shivered. After last night she was through with cypress trees. She had thrown Collin's drawing in her waste basket, but she could not throw off the burden of the boy's secret. Yet she couldn't bear to believe that he was guilty. It would help to talk the whole thing out with Steve; but that, of course, was impossible.

"There's no law that says we have to picnic," Steve remarked. "I could do with a three-inch steak myself."

He pulled up at a restaurant in one of the old Spanish adobe houses in Carmel.

138

"O.K.?" he asked, breaking a long, strained silence.

"O.K." Kathy managed to force her lips into a smile.

Her watch said five o'clock. They were almost alone in the dining room.

Steve gave the order. When the waitress had gone, he leaned across the table and put his hand over Kathy's. "Out with it, Miss Martin. What's wrong?"

How good it would be to confide in Steve! Yet, even to ask advice would be to reveal her patient's confidence. But was there anything wrong in asking a theoretical question?

"I was thinking . . ."

"I noticed that," Steve said a little grimly.

Kathy looked down at her starched uniform. "I thought when I earned the right to wear whites and a stripe on my cap everything would be easy sailing. But suppose you're taking care of somebody who seems like a wonderful person and he's troubled about something. You try to get through to him because the book says you're supposed to see the whole patient—not just his sickness. And you stumble onto a secret that hurts him and other people too. . . ."

"Doctors deal with the 'whole patient' too, don't they, Kathy? A nurse doesn't have the entire job."

Did Steve mean that she ought to tell Dr. McLean that his patient was a fraud and a forger? He'd just say, "Where's your evidence?" Or maybe he'd think Collin was having hallucinations. If that secretary of his let her in to talk to him at all.

"Most doctors don't have time," she said. "Nurses are close to the patients. Bedside nurses, that is."

She was suddenly struck with the many different kinds of nursing—and of nurses. Getting your R.N. was just a beginning. Not everybody, even among her best friends, gave all their attention to patient care. Take Yo, for instance. Even if she hadn't gone on to become a doctor, her interest would have been in conquering disease. She'd probably have gone into a laboratory or become a surgical nurse at the operating table all day like Miss Johnson at San Tomás.

The waitress had brought supper, and Steve was tackling his steak with relish.

"Eat," he commanded.

Kathy nodded, and picked up her knife and fork. "You wouldn't call Jenny a bedside nurse, would you? She's on duty in the whole community. Watches over everybody, the way you guard the forest, Steve. You care about preventing fires or keeping them from spreading, and every tree you look at is part of a forest. That's the way Ramirez is going to be."

"Right now, according to Linda Garfield, Jenny's interest is centered on the postman and whether or not he has a letter from Silver Spoon Junction in his pouch."

Steve threw out this bit of information between bites, obviously glad to have Kathy diverted from her own problem.

"The maintenance man or the girl in the record room are as important to Linda as her patients." Kathy chuckled. "She loves every single person in a hospital. And mothers them all. Before she's back at San Tomás a week, all the student nurses will adore her. Garfield will be a Nursing Arts teacher before Jim gets his M.D."

"What kind of a nurse is Kelley?"

Kathy considered before answering, trying to think of a way to describe Kelley's tremendous creativeness. "Dr. Bowen said once that every day was a separate challenge to Jonesy—like starting a fresh canvas. It's all the same to her whether she's working with babies, or in Surgery or Central Supply."

"And you?" Steve asked, beckoning for more coffee.

"I used to think it was important just to be needed." Kathy blushed. "I guess I cared most about the patients who were most dependent on me. This summer has been so busy that I haven't had time to think whether I'm needed or not. What the patient needs is the most important thing, isn't it?"

"Seems to me I haven't heard about anybody but the Monroe boy."

"I do get sort of involved, don't I? Maybe it was because we saw the accident, Steve. And he's so young and I thought he had such great possibilities." She sighed. "Of course, he's my only patient now. I thought it would be fun to be a private-duty nurse. But that has problems, too. You can get to know too much—things you'd rather forget—things you can't do anything about."

"Now you've got the glooms again," Steve said. "I shouldn't have mumbled his name."

"Oh, Steve, I need your help." Kathy was almost in tears.

"That's the nicest thing you've ever said," Steve answered. "But the person you really need is that kid's doctor."

Would Steve have thought that, Kathy wondered later, if he'd known that Collin Monroe was the criminal Matt was looking for? The boy was waiting for her when she got to the hospital. He was wide awake, bursting to talk.

"It kind of bugs you," he began, "to go to a museum and watch a bunch of cats flip over an 'old master' that you know is as phony as a nine-dollar bill."

Kathy didn't want to hear anything more about the Chinese scroll. Still, as a nurse with her patient's welfare to consider, it was necessary to get Collin to talk.

"How can anybody be sure a thing's phony?"

"There are ways. Take the paper that looks so old. You can get it to look that way if you keep it a few weeks in a place where the fog comes in . . ." The boy suddenly looked at Kathy as if he saw something strange in her face. He clammed up. "I said I wasn't going to talk and I'm not."

"A nurse is a bottomless well," Kathy said. How many student nurses had repeated that cliché straight out of Miss Wilson's lecture on nursing ethics? This time the reassurance failed to work. Kathy tried deliberate provocation. "I don't believe a little sea fog would fool the experts."

Collin gave one of those long, gasping sighs that were a signal of trouble. Kathy went out to the closet where the medicines were kept and prepared a hypo.

When she returned to 202, her patient was wheezing. His eyes were bright and feverish.

"You swear you won't tell?" he whispered. "If you want to see how paper is aged, go up to the summer house. Not inside. Under the house—there's a loose board. You push that away."

"What summer house?"

"Maxfield's."

The strain in his voice brought back sharply Kathy's responsibility as a nurse. She gave him sedation, turned the light low and withdrew to the chair across the room.

"Steve's right," she said to herself. "This is more than I can handle alone."

Next afternoon Kathy sat across from Dr. McLean in his consultation room. The busy man nodded once or twice in agreement while Kathy explained how she had tried to get through to her patient, to discover, if she could, the cause of the emotional disturbance. When she told about the sketch of the cypress tree and the rock, he seemed genuinely interested.

"There may be something in what you say, Miss Martin. Certainly the boy's recovery is slower than I had expected. The complications—the asthma, the slow healing of the fracture—may well be due to mental stress. The body and mind are one. Do you have the drawing with you? I'd like to see it."

However, when she confessed that she had destroyed the picture because of the shocking secret Collin had disclosed, the doctor's manner changed. He smiled incredulously.

"A forger? Not on your life. Edwin Maxfield wouldn't have taken that kind of boy as his *protégé*. Maxfield was too perceptive. I think your point is well taken on the factor of emotional disturbance, Miss Martin. But in my opinion Collin is letting his imagination run away with him—and so are you. He may have heard somewhere this rumor about the Chinese scroll, and he wants to be guilty—guilty of anything, other than Maxfield's death. He's very young, and if you don't mind my saying so, you are young, too, in your profession. I think this projection tends to support your thinking on the basic cause—the etiology—of the slow-healing problem, and I'll have a chat with one of my colleagues in psychiatry. But as to the boy being guilty of forgery—I wouldn't give it another thought. If he raises it again, just take it casually."

It had not occurred to Kathy to doubt Collin's story. What if Dr. McLean were right and the whole thing was a figment of an overwrought imagination? But there was the concrete evidence Collin had offered—the paper, aging under the summer house. What if there was nothing there? Kathy's heart beat fast with the hope. She looked at her watch and then at the Red Cross building across the street. There was time, if she hurried, to get up the hill to Maxfield's home and see for herself. She ran for the bus just stopping at the corner and got on.

XVI

Fog, Footsteps and Forgery

The Maxfield place was back in the hills surrounded, until the last few years, by forests of pine and eucalyptus. A new highway winding through the canyon brought the area within easy reach of the center of town. Kathy had never seen the house, for it was about a quarter of a mile off the highway, but she had noticed Maxfield's name on one of a cluster of mailboxes. She left the bus and set off up a steep, narrow, tree-lined country road. She passed several new houses, all glass and potted palms, then a stretch of untouched woods, hungry for rain. Finally she saw the lush green of lawn and shrubbery, and then the house itself. It was part old, part very modern, and set in a rather formal garden. The windows were boarded up, but the grounds were carefully tended and had recently been watered.

The place was silent as only a deserted house can be. Feeling a little like a ghost, Kathy tiptoed across the grass, past the windowless wall of what seemed to be Edwin Maxfield's studio. She rounded the corner to the north. Here the ground fell abruptly away and a balcony overhung a small ravine. At first she could see nothing but the gray-green tops of acacia trees and a tangle of underbrush and vines. Beyond, far below, was a stretch of ocean.

Kathy started to turn back, to look for the summer house in some other direction, when her eyes rested on a few roughly placed stones that might serve as steps. Gingerly she tried the top step. It was steadier than it looked. Three more steps down, a turn, and a circular, rustic roof came into view. Under the summer house, Collin had said. There the fog could do its work. The damp gray fingers of the fog were already rising from the water.

Kathy pushed through a mass of dark red bougainvillea and found her way stopped by posts holding up the porch roof of the summer house. Boards again, rather carelessly nailed on to the sagging posts.

She put her hand out to balance herself on the uneven ground, and the board gave way with a crackle and fell sideways into the bougainvillea. "There's a loose board," Collin had said. His directions had been clear and exact.

"When I stoop down I'll see the sheets of paper being prepared for more forgeries—more cheating." Kathy almost wished she hadn't come. The possibility that she could persuade the boy to confess his crime seemed remote and unrealistic. That Matt or anyone else would unearth the facts without assistance, remoter still. She wasn't even sure she wanted Collin's secret discovered. She was bitterly disappointed in him, but he was unhappy enough without further punishment.

A glance at the open space under the summer house floor confirmed that the evidence Collin offered was no dream. Long sheets of paper were suspended like laundry on a clothesline. Spider webs delicately festooned the edges of several sheets. The fine layer of dust raised by the falling board had not yet settled.

Kathy made no effort to enter the hiding place. She had seen enough. Heavy-hearted, she bent down to put the loose board back in place. At this moment, she heard a noise overhead.

Wood rats in the summer house? The sound was too regular and heavy. Kathy's hands trembled. She had difficulty replacing the plank. It slid out of her fingers and fell against a rock. She held her breath and listened.

There was the sound again. The papers moved with the vibration. No wood rat or any other small creature made a noise like that. Nothing did, but human footsteps. Someone was in the summer house—someone watching her through the cracks in the boarding.

Kathy found herself running, stumbling, short of breath. The tangle of vines and shrubs which had seemed so picturesque was now her enemy. Loose stones rose up and blocked her path.

She had almost gained the clear, smooth stretch of lawn when she twisted her ankle and fell.

"I'm all right. It's broad daylight. There was nothing to be afraid of. It could have been the gardener or—or anybody in the summer house." Kathy's panic had vanished. Chagrin had taken the place of fear. "Now my uniform's a mess and I'll be late to my class."

But when she pulled herself to a standing position, she winced with pain. Resting her weight on her left foot and holding on to an overhanging branch, she managed to reach the top step and the open lawn. She sank down on the step. For a moment she did nothing but stare dumbly at her right foot as if, for all the throbbing pain, it didn't belong to her at all. Then, methodically, she unlaced her shoe and rubbed her ankle.

A sprain or a break? Only an X ray could tell that. Under her fingers she could feel the foot begin to swell.

Her stocking was torn by brambles, and a few ugly scratches showed through.

"Another pair of stockings shot," she said and winced again as she tried to stand.

No one was in sight to help her, and the memory of the footsteps that had frightened her made her hesitate to call. The foot had swelled so much that she couldn't get her shoe on.

There was nothing to do but hobble to the nearest house. Even the distance across the lawn seemed farther than she could go. She was weak and dizzy by the time she came to the road.

"And it's a quarter of a mile to the main highway!" she thought mournfully, when she had limped another hundred yards. She sat down on a boulder by the lonely roadside to rest and massaged her ankle again. She was trying to decide whether to tear her petticoat to make a bandage when a car backed out of the driveway of one of the houses ahead.

Kathy called, thinking, "They'll never hear me." She could see the driver hesitate and peer over his shoulder. She hobbled to the road and waved her shoe like a flag. The car eased out into the road and backed slowly up the hill.

Tears of relief and pain ran down Kathy's cheeks as a gray-haired man helped her into the back seat of the car, and the gloved and hatted woman in the front seat made sympathetic noises.

"I was taking a walk," Kathy murmured, "and fell. Believe me, I'll never say *just* a sprained ankle to a patient again," she added ruefully. "I never knew a sprain could hurt so."

"You poor thing! Shall we take you to the County Hospital? I suppose you work there," the woman added.

The way she glanced at the cap and uniform made Kathy realize that she must look a fright. Hastily she straightened her cap.

"No, I'm on private duty. At Ocean Cliff. But if the County Hospital's not too far out of your way . . . Someone at First Aid will bandage the ankle, and I can phone from there."

There'd be simply no way to explain what she was doing on a lonely mountain road instead of being at her Red Cross course. And Dr. McLean would have to order another nurse for Collin Monroe—if he could get one this late. And she'd never have a chance to convince Collin that he ought to confess and take the consequences. And she couldn't even hint to Matt and Gail about the hidden store of paper.

"Here we are." The driver of the car interrupted Kathy's doleful thoughts. They were at the emergency entrance of a large hospital.

"Kathy Martin! What on earth . . . ?" The nurse at the reception desk had a San Tomás stripe on her cap. She had been a Junior when Kathy was a Probie in Nursing School. Peggy Malone was her name. Kathy hadn't known Peggy terribly well, but it was wonderful to have her take over now.

It was Peggy who brought her an aspirin and a cup of hot tea. It was Peggy who rolled her in a wheel chair to the X-ray room and chattered about Miss Covington and the old days at Nursing School while the good-looking young intern bandaged Kathy's ankle. It was Peggy who phoned Mrs. Smith and then called Mr. Martin to come down and take Kathy home. Mrs. Smith had thought that the best solution. She promised to send Kathy's clothes. It was Peggy, finally, who borrowed a pillow from the hospital for her to rest her throbbing foot on, in the front seat of the pickup, and stood waving them off in the night.

"Why do you look so gloomy, daughter?" Mr. Martin asked as they went up the ramp to the freeway. "That doctor said your ankle would be O.K. in a few days. You know that a sprained ankle is nothing serious."

"I know, Papa. It feels quite comfortable already. It's just—I was on private duty taking care of that young boy who was hurt in the accident and now I'm off the case."

"So? Is my Kathy the only nurse at that hospital?"

"He needs me, Papa," Kathy said earnestly—and then she stopped short. The reason she felt especially needed was part of Collin's secret. Not even to her father could she reveal it.

XVII

Byline: Christopher Matthews

"Three guesses what I brought you, Kathy!" Johnny bounded into the living room with one hand behind his back.

When his sister first came home to nurse her sprained ankle, he insisted that his school ought to declare a holiday so that he could take care of her. The school authorities failed to cooperate, so Johnny compromised by dashing home with a daily surprise the moment classes were dismissed. No leading man in an old-fashioned musical comedy made a more dramatic entrance than Johnny contrived day after day.

Kathy loved it. "Another kitten?" she guessed.

He had brought a scrawny calico cat home the first day. The animal fortunately had taken itself away after enjoying a dish of chocolate ice cream.

Johnny shook his head. "I asked a lady for a pretty little kitten, but she said its eyes weren't open yet."

"A model airplane for us to fix?"

Johnny's presents were not always selected without a hint of self-interest. He collected model airplanes along with his mountains of baseball cards.

Kathy wrinkled her brow in thought. Yesterday's chameleon was resting on a begonia leaf in a pot on the end table. The leaf was both red and green and the poor reptile was practically having a nervous breakdown trying to camouflage its color. Chameleons were rare. It was unlikely that Johnny had found another one.

"It begins with an L," Johnny said.

"A lizard?"

"Nope," his hand came out with a letter. " 'Miss Katherina Martin'—it's easy as pie to read."

"It's from Gail," Kathy said, slitting the envelope. "You remember her—I went to her wedding."

"Sure. Was she a bridesmaid, too?"

Kathy laughed. "She was the bride."

"Like on T.V.? There was a man took a bribe and the sheriff hauled him off to jail."

"What? Yes, I guess so . . ." Kathy wasn't listening to Johnny. She was absorbed in the contents of Gail's note and the clipping enclosed. Matt's first by-line! Eagerly she read on:

The paper expert, Mr. Harper, says the scroll is fraudulent. The counterfeiters made the paper out of rice fibers on a hand press, just the way the old paper was made. He snipped a corner off the bottom of the scroll, where it fits into the frame. The fibers, examined under a microscope, showed differences from the material in Chinese paper. In fact, the fibers seem to come from a new hybrid rice plant grown only in Arkansas, USA . . .

A clever imitation and remarkably aged, Mr. Harper says. Short of chemical analysis he can't be a hundred percent sure, but Matt's boss was convinced that there is something to Mr. Ho's contention and gave Matt a green light to raise the question.

Such excitement all day! The curator and the art dealer are threatening to sue each other, and both of them are threatening to sue the newspaper. And Matt is looking under orange crates to find the artist. Where do we go from here?

Kathy groaned. "Where do we go? Right to Collin Monroe's hospital bed . . ."

She was terribly disappointed in Collin, but couldn't help being torn with sympathy for his plight. If only she were still on the case she might persuade him to come forward with his story. Matt could make it much easier for him that way. Without Collin's permission she could not even explain to Matt the emotional conditions involved.

Kathy fretted the afternoon through and had worked herself into quite a state when Steve stopped by after work to see if she wanted to go for a drive.

"The Lone Ranger! Just in time to save the day!" Kathy jumped up, ignoring the twinge in her ankle. "Steve, take

me down to see Collin Monroe! There's no reason I can't
go as a visitor. We can take him apples—Pop started picking Newtowns today."

"I haven't seen you so pepped up since the time we dou-
ble-dated Matt and Gail," Steve said. "What's the idea?"

"It's about them—sort of." Kathy fished out Gail's letter and the clipping from among the pile of paperbacks
on the table. "You read these while I get into a dress, but
don't ask me any more questions because—" Kathy bit
her lips. "I hate professional secrets," she said as she
limped from the room.

An hour later, she walked into Ocean Cliff Hospital
with a basket of pale-green apples—her excuse for visiting
the boy who had been her patient.

Dr. McLean frowned. "The prognosis is not too favor-
station.

"Miss Martin! I've been wanting to see you."

"I hope my giving up the Monroe case wasn't too inconvenient, Doctor. How is he?"

Dr. McLean frowned. "The prognosis is not too favor-
able. Symptoms about the same. I've been wanting to talk
to you. I've about come around to your way of thinking.
If there is something more than just the accident on that
boy's mind—if what he told you was based on reality—
it could account for a good deal of his trouble."

Kathy might have been just a visitor in her gay plaid
jumper and a gift in her hand, but her manner was suddenly very professional—the manner of an R.N. confer-
ring with a physician.

"The forgery wasn't a projection of Collin's imagination," she said slowly. "I have some concrete evidence." She told about the hidden store of paper in the Maxfield summer house, and then produced the newspaper clipping. "Christopher Matthews, who wrote this story, is a friend of mine."

McLean ran his fingers through his hair, deep in thought.

"There are occasions, if the welfare of the patient is at stake, when a professional confidence must be revealed. I'd like to see that paper in the summer house—maybe confront the young rascal with a piece of it. Get him to talk. And if he doesn't. . . ."

"I could show you the paper now, Dr. McLean." Kathy's eyes were shining. "It's not far in a car."

"Take your apples in to Collin. I'll wait. It might cheer the boy up to see you."

Kathy rejoined Dr. McLean almost at once, explaining that Collin was dozing. "I just left the apples and scribbled a note on a jot sheet," she said.

Steve came toward them when they walked out of the door.

Kathy stammered over the introductions. How could she explain to Steve? Collin's confession was still a professional secret—not hers to give away!

Dr. McLean seemed to have guessed the source of her embarrassment, for he said very casually, "I'll take my car too and lead the way to the Maxfield place. You can explain to your young man what the problem is."

They were hardly out of the driveway before Kathy had told Steve the whole story.

"You don't know what a relief it is to talk about it, Steve."

"Let me get this straight," Steve said. "As soon as Dr. McLean sees the evidence with his own eyes, he's going to let you tell Matt?"

Kathy nodded, suddenly sobered. "The whole thing will be out of my hands then. It will be rough for Collin, but it's the only way he'll get well."

"He's young, of course—he'll have time to live this down. But it beats me how a youngster could plan and carry through a deal like that."

"That's the sad part, Steve. And I thought at first he was just a sweet, sensitive kid. Even when he confessed I couldn't believe it, at first. It wasn't until I saw the paper hanging there—ready for more forgeries."

McLean turned off the highway and up the hill. Steve followed and drew up behind the doctor's car in the Maxfield driveway.

"You stay in the car, young lady," McLean said, "and take care of that ankle. Kovak and I will find the summer house. Over in that ravine, facing the ocean, you said?"

Kathy wasn't sorry to be left behind. She had no desire to see the summer house again. The fall had been a frightening experience . . . to be in such pain there alone. *Had* she been there alone? The unexplained footsteps still puzzled her.

It seemed no time at all before the two men returned,

coming toward her across the lawn. They were walking very slowly—and McLean was empty-handed.

"I thought you were going to bring some of the paper back with you," Kathy said. "You found the summer house, didn't you?"

"We found it all right." Steve held out a scrap of torn paper, a jagged triangular fragment. Tough but smooth. She knew just how it felt. She had seen a scrap of paper like that before—in Collin's hand at the time of the accident, when she bent over his broken body to stanch the wound.

"We found the place and pulled away the loose board. This is all that was left under the summer house. Nothing there but dirt and spiders," Steve said.

"The paper's gone?" Kathy was startled. "But I saw the long strips hanging from the rafters and spider webs all over them."

Steve said, "Monroe must have gotten somebody to take the paper away, Kathy."

"The spider webs were plentiful," Dr. McLean said grimly. "There's no doubt, Miss Martin, that your information is correct. The dust marks on the clothesline are evidence enough. Let me know when your newspaper friend can come. I want to be present when he talks to Collin."

The doctor drove off, in a great hurry as usual, and Steve and Kathy started north toward Appleton.

Steve said, "Somebody took that paper from under the summer house. It can't be Maxfield. And the boy is in a body cast. So obviously there's a third person in this counterfeit deal."

"Who?" Kathy sounded tired and discouraged. The opportunity she had fought for had come, and she wasn't sure that she wanted it.

"Whatever's going on, as soon as you notify Matt, you're out of it, Kathy. But I suspect Matt's going to have more of a story than he bargained for."

XVIII

Collin Monroe's Secret

The next afternoon, two cars rolled up to the Ocean Cliff parking lot. Dr. McLean edged his shabby blue Chevy into a space reserved for doctors. Steve pulled up beside him, and five young people piled out—he and Kathy and Kelley from the front and Matt and Gail from the back seat. They were a subdued lot. This was not a gala excursion.

"We'll be waiting in the cove," Steve said as Kathy and Matt followed the doctor to the hospital door.

McLean turned to Matt as the three entered the medical wing. "I didn't mention that a stranger would be with us," he explained, "merely that Miss Martin would be in the neighborhood and would drop in to see him. He reacted rather violently to this information, and we gave him a sedative. It should just be wearing off."

161

Matt nodded. They were outside Room 202 now.

"I hope I did the right thing wearing my uniform," Kathy whispered nervously. "Collin is used to me as his nurse."

"Quite right," the doctor said. "Just go in as you normally would, without knocking. We'll wait outside until you open the door."

Kathy put on a smile for her entrance. The book said, "A pleasing personality in a nurse is very important—you must be cheerful, poised and sympathetic at all times . . ." Even, she thought, with butterflies in your stomach, when you're about to ask your patient to confess to being a cheat and a forger!

"Hi, Collin! Did you have a good sleep?"

She was shocked at his appearance. He made no effort to answer, though his deep-set eyes followed her as she moved around the room. She opened the curtains, rearranged the flowers and knickknacks on the bureau, and continued to talk in a conversational tone.

"You've added a zebra to your collection. Pretty cool!" There was still no response. She tried the gambit of surprise. "A friend of mine has come to see you, Collin. He's hip on Chinese painting. I thought you might like to talk to him."

She opened the door. Matt walked in and calmly took the chair by the bed. Dr. McLean stood just in the doorway out of the patient's narrow range of vision.

"This is Christopher Matthews," Kathy said quietly. "He is interested in the scroll in the San Francisco museum. Wouldn't you like to tell him what you know about it?"

"I don't know anything about it!" Collin's voice rose shrilly. He twisted his head on the pillow and his breathing became shallow and noisy. Kathy tensed. *Not again!* she thought. Then, slowly, Collin seemed to relax.

"All right, so Max stole the name of another artist. But he was going to make it right. I swear he was. He promised." Sobs came from deep in the boy's throat. A minute passed before he continued. "He could have given the money back. You see that, don't you? If that steering rod hadn't snapped . . ."

Kathy dropped to her knees by the bed and put her hand on Collin's shoulder. "Do you mean that Edwin Maxfield forged the name of Chon Fang on the scroll he painted? Is that what you're trying to tell us, Collin? You didn't have anything to do with it at all?"

"What do you take me for? Max was teaching me to paint in oils. He'd sketch in the landscape—ocean, rocks, cypress—the kind of thing he was famous for. After the sketch was made I'd finish the painting. Max said that's what apprentices did for all the old masters."

Matt leaned forward. "If you didn't have anything to do with the forgery, how did you know about the paper?"

Collin's words came swiftly now, tumbling one over the other. "In the summer house? I hung it there myself —Max showed me how. That's the kind of cool cat he was. He was conducting an experiment in brush work— that's what he said. I'd bring up a sheet and stretch it on the floor and get out his inks and all. He'd be sitting there cross-legged in a white kimono thing, leaning on one elbow with the brush held like this. Recapturing a lost art, he called it, and searching for truth. Searching for a way to make a fast buck, that's what it really was."

"Who got rid of the paper for you?" Matt asked.

The boy lifted his head from the pillow. A bewildered look came into his eyes. "Is the paper gone? It doesn't matter, does it? Not with Maxfield dead. . . ." He appealed to Kathy.

"When he sold the painting to that sea captain—you must have known the truth then," Matt insisted.

"What sea captain? I didn't know what had become of the thing until the day of the accident. We had been to the museum and there was this show piece. 'Ninth Century. Chon Fang,' the card said. But I had *seen* Max working on it. Using this precious paper he'd managed to get hold of."

"You couldn't be sure, could you, Collin?" Kathy asked.

Collin nodded. Tears came into his eyes again. "I'm sure. On the way home I asked him. He—he laughed and said what people didn't know wouldn't hurt them, and where did I think he got the money to send his sister to Italy and board me all summer for nothing? Did customers pay thousands of dollars for cypress trees—or for anything else painted by a living artist? He reached into the back seat and pulled out a roll of paper and said for me to choose a good Chinese name and he'd let me in on the racket. Just to shut me up."

"What did you say then, Collin?" Kathy asked gently.

"I was pretty frantic. I always thought Max was too much. Really too much. Practically a god. I snatched the paper away and threw it out of the car. That's when he blew up. 'What do you want to do? Ruin me?' he said. I didn't answer, just kept looking straight ahead at the road. Then Max said that maybe he could give the money back. I could tell he meant it. He wasn't just saying it to string me along. It was as though he'd had to make that Chinese painting—as though he didn't really want to do it. And then the accident happened. . . . I made up my mind not to tell anybody. I don't know how I came to spill it to you."

The doctor signaled them. His patient had had enough. Matt stood up.

"It's tough, Collin, having to find out some of the things people are driven to do. But I'll say this—you had a good teacher. That scroll is a fraud on the public, but just for what it is, it's a thing of beauty. And we'd have found out somehow even if you hadn't told us."

Collin didn't look up when they left. His face was half buried in the pillow.

Dr. McLean walked beside Kathy to the door. "Collin Monroe will be grateful to you some day. They say you learn by living. The boy has had more than his share of learning these past weeks. Now it's behind him."

Kathy sniffed and fumbled for a Kleenex. "I'm so happy for Collin," she said. "How could I have suspected a boy like that?"

The doctor grunted. "You would have found it twice as hard to suspect Ed Maxfield, if you'd known him. I don't understand it. I happen to know something about his financial affairs. He didn't get rich on this counterfeiting deal."

On the beach, Gail and Kelley had gathered driftwood and built a fire. The plan was to picnic by the ocean and then drive back to the Martin ranch. There, Matt could work up the rough draft of his story and check any missing details before going back to the city.

Both girls were silent and preoccupied as they sat watching the blue flames die to embers. They were worried about Kathy. She had walked into the hospital as if she were going to her own funeral.

"If only Martin wouldn't get so involved in her patients' problems," Gail said. "It's rough on a nurse having to give away a professional secret."

Kelley poked the fire. "Just right for the steak," she said without enthusiasm. "After all, it was the doctor's decision."

Gail nodded. "And Matt will be as gentle as he can. Collin Monroe is just a boy after all—even if he did pull as shrewd a deal as any I've ever heard of."

"What I don't get is how—"

"How Kathy got the little punk to talk?" Gail asked. "It wasn't anything she planned."

"That isn't what I was thinking about—but never mind . . ." Her eyes were on Steve who had done nothing but pace the sand. "I wonder if his watch has a second hand?" she said. "If he's looked at it once, he's looked at it fifty times since Kathy went through the hospital door."

"Hey! They must be coming!" Gail jumped up, as Steve started with long strides across the beach.

"He didn't do it, Steve! It wasn't what I thought at all!" Kathy's voice was jubilant.

"Watch your ankle," Steve called. "Wait there!" He scrambled up the steep path. "I'm going to carry you."

"Steve, you can't. I weigh a ton."

"I'm not a fireman for nothing," Steve answered firmly.

Gail and Matt were walking across the beach hand in hand, talking a mile a minute. Kelley surveyed the scene drily and opened the picnic hamper.

"I might as well put on the steak," she said. "Nobody's making any sense."

"Make it a fast lunch, girls," Matt said after Kathy had repeated Collin's story for a second time. "I've got to get to a phone. If a totally unknown boy had done the forgery I could have taken my time on the story. Edwin Maxfield makes it front-page stuff."

"Are you sure about the facts?" Gail stopped buttering rolls. There was a frown on her face.

"What's on your mind, Mrs. Sherlock?" Matt was all attention. He had great respect for Gail's hunches.

"Well—" Gail spoke hesitantly. She didn't want to upset any applecarts. "I know it's more plausible for a fine artist like Maxfield to have painted the scroll, even if it isn't in his usual style. But Maxfield *is* dead and Kathy's patient has had time to reconsider his sickroom confession."

"Gail!" Kathy cried. "Collin didn't confess to anything. It was just my stupidity."

"I'm sorry, Martin. But suppose the boy wanted to get out of it. The easiest thing to do would be to pin it on a dead man. Especially when the paper was stored at the Maxfield house in the first place. When he realized that the paper might give him away, he could have gotten some school friend to get rid of it. That was the only real evidence pointing to his own guilt, wasn't it?"

"I thought of that," Matt answered. "I tried to think up a trick question to check him. I remembered the smuggler from Hong Kong. I figured whoever painted the picture must have used the sea captain as a go-between —to plant the thing. I asked the boy point-blank. It was obvious he had never heard of the guy."

Kelley interrupted. "You don't know why I asked to come along, Gail. It was because I was sure there was something funny about Collin's story. An artist—a good one—in whatever century—painted that scroll. Not an untrained amateur seventeen years old!"

Gail cast an appealing glance in Kathy's direction. She hated to raise these questions, but it was absolutely necessary to get at the truth. "Another thing," she said. "It's funny that Gray never murmured a word about Maxfield."

"Why should he? He already had one dead man to blame," Matt said.

"Gray?" Kathy looked bewildered.

Kelley gave a short laugh. "Our own Amos X. Gray, Martin. He's the art dealer who's caught in this net."

"Gray claims to have bought the painting from this sea captain and sold it to the museum?" Steve asked abruptly. He had been serving steak sandwiches and had taken no part in the conversation. "You couldn't question the man, Matt, as I remember it, because of his sudden death in a lumber camp. Do you know the date of this smuggler's death?"

"What are you driving at, Steve?" Matt asked, as he leafed through a note book. "Here it is—the clipping from the paper, dated Wednesday, September 15."

"Three days after our wedding," Gail announced.

"What day did Gray consent to give you the information?"

Matt thought back. "Let's see. It was on Sunday of that week. My day off. Somebody phoned from the office —said I had a special delivery. By jiminy! I get the drift of your questions, Steve. Gray didn't accuse the fellow until after he was dead!"

Steve nodded. "He could have picked a name at random out of the obituary column."

"Amos Gray is a victim of the fraud himself, Steve," Kelley said. "He's sold rare art objects for years to museums and private collections over the country. It's hard on him to have been taken in by a fraud."

"My heart bleeds for Mr. Gray," Steve retorted. "But if I were an art collector and had bought any old masters

from him lately, I'd have them checked pretty thoroughly. There's the matter of the paper, too, in Maxfield's
summer house. Somebody made that paper and brought
it to Maxfield and somebody took it away! Why wouldn't
the art dealer be the logical accomplice?"

Matt jumped up and began packing up the food and
utensils. "Eat up," he ordered. "I want to get to a phone."

Kathy remembered the scroll in Gray's shop. "It was
in a locked case, Jonesy. And he called it a collector's
item."

"Fourteenth century—I remember. What about it?"

"I was wondering," Kathy said slowly, "whether it was
counterfeit or real."

"Mr. Ho would be able to tell—if he could get his hands
on it," Matt said.

Gail closed the hamper and threw the coffee they
hadn't had time to drink on the dying embers.

"Aren't detectives allowed a cup of coffee?" Steve
groaned. "I wish I'd kept my questions to myself."

"I'll buy you some coffee in a drive-in, while Matt
phones our Chinese friend," Gail said. Her eyes sparkled
with excitement. "What a story Matt will have, if Gray's
scroll turns out to be counterfeit!"

XIX

On a Mountain Road

There was a stillness over the Martin orchard, a feel of autumn in the sunset, as Steve's car rolled up the drive. A few late red apples hung on the branches, and Mrs. Martin's garden was lavish with color. But the brilliance of the blossoms, the splendor of the setting sun, were overshadowed by the muted greens and browns of the trees and meadow, and the sky was misty gray.

Kelley gave a sigh of pleasure and took her time getting out of the car. The subdued light would be a challenge to a painter.

"Can you smell the autumn, Matt? Isn't it heavenly here?" Gail said.

But Matt was too tense to catch the relaxed mood of the others. His ears were tuned for the ring of the telephone. Two hours had gone by since he had spoken to

171

Mr. Ho in San Francisco, time enough for the old man to have examined the scroll in Gray's studio. Mr. Ho had promised to call him at the Martins' with a report.

They had not come directly to Appleton, but had stopped instead at the Maxfield place. Kathy had led the way past the boarded-up residence to the summer house in the ravine. Matt had crawled under the summer house —which Kelley insisted upon calling a gazebo—and had come out dusty but triumphant. He had found another small fragment of paper, enough for a chemical analysis. Without touching the clothesline, for fear of erasing fingerprints, he had counted ten dust-free spaces where the sheets of paper had hung.

The paper and its disappearance suddenly seemed all-important. The person or persons who removed it must be found. The purpose may have been chiefly to conceal evidence of Maxfield's forgery. This was Gail's opinion. But Kathy had pointed out that ten well-aged sheets provided material for future forgeries, and Matt was inclined to agree.

Mr. Ho's telephone call might be of immediate importance. If the scroll in Amos Gray's gallery were counterfeit, the search for Maxfield's accomplice would be ended almost before it started. If not, then "the paper chase" might prove long and arduous.

"Come out of that brown study, Mr. Sherlock," Kathy called. "There's been a phone call for you. Nobody's home, but Mom left a note. They've gone to Johnny's P.T.A."

While Matt dialed the long distance operator, the others gathered at the kitchen table, frankly eavesdropping. They could make little of Matt's end of the long conversation, however. He seemed slightly disappointed when he put down the phone.

"Mr. Ho examined the scroll in the case. It's sixteenth century, not fourteenth, but it's the genuine article."

"I'm not surprised," Kelley said. "I thought you were all off the beam in suspecting Mr. Gray."

"I don't know if we are or not," Matt answered. "Ho had the impression that something had been moved from the case. It seemed as if an exchange of scrolls might have been made rather hastily."

"Why didn't he ask Gray, then and there?" Gail asked.

"He couldn't. The shop was empty."

"Mr. Gray goes to his Santa Cruz mountain retreat several days a week," Kelley explained, still on the defensive.

"I'd taken the precaution of sending a police detective with Mr. Ho. When no one answered the bell, he used a pass key. It's a good thing I did. They had a little trouble with a young man in a Roman toga."

"Oh! Yes!" Kathy said. "He served us tea."

"The detective explained that he'd heard a curious noise and had come in to investigate. It was perfectly legal," Matt added with a sheepish grin.

Gail leaned forward. "You remember a lot of details about that gallery, don't you, Martin?"

Kathy nodded.

"You wrote me about a fourteenth-century scroll. Did you get your centuries mixed?"

"No, I didn't. It *was* a fourteenth-century scroll we saw. Wasn't it, Kelley?"

Kelley sat with her chin pressed against both fists in deep thought. "It was," she said slowly. "And the one now in the case was painted two hundred years later. There's nothing rare about a sixteenth-century scroll from China. The European galleries are full of them." She turned to Matt. "I—I could be wrong about Mr. Gray. I'd get to town and have a talk with him if I were you."

"We'd be on the freeway now if it would do any good," Matt answered. "Ho and the police detective made an informal call at Gray's house on Nob Hill. The detective figured the whole setup was a little too smooth. The butler wouldn't let them in. Said Gray had gone to his mountain retreat for meditation and was not to be disturbed. Someplace near Loma Prieta, he thought."

"Meditation!" Steve snorted and pulled out his fire marshall's map. He drew a wide circle around Loma Prieta, the highest peak in the Santa Cruz mountains. "These are the Ranger stations in that area," he said, pointing to four widely separated stars. "Gray's retreat must be fairly well out of the way of the stations or I'd have seen it."

"What's the idea?" Matt asked.

"You want that interview, don't you? It might as well take place tonight." Steve handed the map to Gail and stood up. "Study the roads so you can direct the driver.

Matt, you don't mind some rough going, do you? Kathy and I will take the freeway to Coyote and hit the north area. You follow Mt. Madonna Road up past the Ranger station. Explore every dirt road from there on. You can keep in touch at any of the Ranger stations. My car is in contact with all of them."

There were not many roads up in the northern mountains, and Steve knew them all. Kathy sat back confidently with Steve at the wheel. It was only eight o'clock, but the nights were getting long. It had been dark for an hour. Collin Monroe would be getting his second sleeping pill—if he needed one. If the psychotherapy books were right, his emotional tension ought to be relieved after he'd put his secret into Matt's hands.

The car radio was wide open. Two Rangers were hamming in a carefree fashion.

"Those guys get lonesome," Steve explained, when a chuckle told him Kathy was listening in. "They yak-yak half the night." Suddenly the clowning stopped. A message came in a kind of professional jargon.

Steve listened intently. "There's smoke in Area 20," he interpreted. "That's northeast of us." He stopped and flashed a light on a small map posted on his dashboard. "Any personnel in the area are requested to inspect at once." He glanced at Kathy a little anxiously. "I'm not on duty," he began.

"But you think you ought to go?" Kathy said. She would have preferred to go on with the original plan, but she recognized that firemen, like doctors and nurses, were never completely off duty.

"The area is about a mile off the road from this side. A car can get through on a sort of cow path. It's kind of rough going on the edge of a ravine," he added doubtfully. "I could let you wait at the Ranger station."

"That would waste time," Kathy said. "Let's get going."

Steve shifted gears and stepped on the gas. Kathy could see that this was work he loved. The bumps and twists set her ankle throbbing, but she braced herself and determined to enjoy the wild ride.

"There's the smoke!" she cried, after five minutes of pure torture. "Over on the left. It's coming from a cabin. Steve! Look! A car's pulling away."

Steve jerked up the radio mouthpiece. "Kovak reporting. Mountain cabin on fire—Area Twelve-A, twenty, seventeen. Ranger Station Ten, watch for blue car headed east."

He stopped the car and rushed for his emergency extinguisher in the trunk.

"Got some experimental chemicals in here—we'll see how they work," he said, and ducked into the building.

Kathy sat quite still, biting her lips to keep from screaming. Once or twice in Appleton she had seen Steve at fires. Then there'd been fire trucks and crowds. Here, he was all alone. He could be burned. He could swallow smoke. Or suppose those experimental chemicals blew up the house. Kathy distrusted experiments she knew nothing about.

Steve had the small blaze under control when a small fire truck pulled up. The driver tugged at a hose.

Kathy was surprised to see another car close behind. Matt, Gail and Kelley jumped out.

"Where's Steve?" Matt called.

Kathy pointed to the cabin.

At this moment Steve appeared on top of the low roof. The searchlight from the fire truck was squarely on him. His face was streaked with soot, his good clothes a mess, but even Kathy could see that he was having a wonderful time.

"This one doesn't amount to much," the uniformed fireman said. "Nothing but paper burning up—watch those red cinders."

He began rolling up his hose. In a minute he trotted past with an extinguisher over his shoulder. In ten minutes the fire was out.

Kathy suddenly remembered the car that had driven away so furtively.

"Kelley! Do you know what kind of car Gray drives?"

"I do," Matt said. "It's a blue Cadillac."

"We saw it!" Kathy cried. "At least, we saw a blue car drive over the hill as we came up."

"Martin luck!" Kelley said. "It must be his cabin. We had just about given up."

Matt made a rush for the door.

"Is it O.K. to come in?" he shouted.

"If the girls don't mind ruining a pair of shoes," Steve answered. "Watch out for charred paper. It's hot."

"It *is* the hideout!" Gail rushed in ahead of the others. "That's a press, a real old kind. And the pans for soaking the fibers! Matt, he did more than steal the paper from Maxfield—he made it himself! Can't you see the headlines in the late edition?" She threw her arms around her husband.

"Don't rush it, Mrs. Sherlock," Kathy said. She was as excited as Gail and had gone poking around the cabin, forgetful of her ankle. "There are still some loose ends to mop up."

"You're mixing your metaphors, Miss Martin," Matt said. He bent over and pushed a pile of debris away from broken pieces of plaster cast. Matt held up one fragment larger than the rest, clearly an ear and a part of a cheek and jaw.

"It's what's left from the casting of a piece of bronze sculpture," Kelley said, a little sadly. "I expect Chinese scrolls were only one of Mr. Gray's artful experiments." She picked up a scrap of blackened paper that had fluttered near her foot. A character from the Chinese alphabet was still visible in an unburned corner. "Look how beautiful it is! Why would a man who appreciated beautiful things as much as Amos Gray did stoop to lying and cheating?"

"For money," Kathy answered. "Don't feel too sorry for your art lover, Jonesy. He was a phony."

"Kathy's right," Matt said firmly. "If he had to get rich to keep himself in luxury, I'd rather he had robbed a bank."

XX

"Our Orders Have Come"

Gail had written to Kathy:

Come to our first anniversary party. We'll be married a month next Sunday. If you must bring presents make it old shoes.

Private-eye Merry Mason will have no truck with counterfeits. He will accept only genuine antiques and finds the white polish on nursing shoes especially delectable. Merry's choice may be a protest against my studying for State Boards instead of playing ball with him.

Matt sends his best, or would if he knew I was writing you. I never see the man. I'm a front-page widow. But I'll put him on leash for the party.

Kathy and Steve were the first to arrive at the Matthews' apartment. She was wearing a new, blue wool dress, high heels and gloves.

"Nobody would guess you're a hick from the back country," Gail said admiringly. "Come in and catch your breath. Matt's not home, naturally. I had him safely roped to the chair all morning. Then an hour ago, the telephone rang. . . ."

Steve laughed. "Looks as if you've married a fireman."

"Except that he sets the blaze himself." Gail led the way to the big front room and stood expectantly waiting for them to notice all the changes.

Cushions had replaced all but one of the orange crates, and it held a record player. Curtains of pale-green Chinese silk hung at the windows. There was a bowl of red roses on the coffee table.

"Matt got a raise," Gail said, and dragged Kathy over to a bulletin board covered with clippings. "There's the whole story from beginning to end! There's a warrant out for Gray's arrest. He'll be charged with arson and blackmail."

"I get the arson charge," Steve said. "I can testify that the fire in the cabin was no accident. But how do you figure selling a painting under false claims is blackmail?"

The slam of the front door interrupted them, and Matt came bounding in with Yo. "Here's something I found on the doorstep," he said. "She might be a little out of breath, keeping up with me. I was in a hurry," he said to Gail. "I like to pay my debts promptly," and he gave her a kiss.

Gail's eyes sparkled. "I bet him two kisses for one that the phone call meant they've arrested Amos X. Gray."

"And you were so right," Matt paced the room in excitement. "He got as far as New York. Had a plane ticket for Rome in his pocket."

Matt nodded. "It's quite a story. Artists of talent were the real victims. We can get back the money, but for years he has had half a dozen artists under contract for their total output under his direction."

"I don't understand," Yo said. "It's hard for an artist to make a living. To be under contract to sell all you paint . . . is that bad?"

"They had to produce just what he ordered. I guess it looked good to the poor fellows at first. Some, like Maxfield, jumped at the chance to be free of money worries, to have a chance to create things of real beauty. But the contract and the funds he advanced kept them in his debt. It must have been hard, practically impossible, to break away by the time Maxfield found out what 'under Gray's direction' really meant."

"He trapped other artists by threats," Gail said. "Tell them about the sculptor, Matt."

"The man had once escaped from prison. Gray knew it and threatened to expose him if he refused to do the fake antique statues. He's been blackmailing him for money ever since."

"The Roman emperor!" Kathy cried.

"Exactly, Dr. Watson." Gail was in her element. "Matt's story about Maxfield's Chinese scroll gave the sculptor the courage to confess."

Kathy stooped down to read the last newspaper clip-

ping. "You didn't mention how you got the story, Matt,"
she said gratefully.

"Didn't need to. Edwin Maxfield's painting started it
all, but Maxfield is dead and Gray was forced to give
back the $10,000 the museum paid."

"Then Collin won't have to testify?"

"There'd be no reason to call him at all," Matt reas-
sured her.

Kathy beamed with happiness. "It's too much—really
too much, as Collin would say. It will wipe the last
anxiety from his mind. He can throw all his energies into
getting well."

Gail explained to Yo, "Martin's going in for psychotherapy in a big way. And it seems to have worked. A
case of emotional disturbance preventing a fracture
repair."

Kathy blushed and fumbled in her handbag for a letter from Collin's mother. "He's home and won't be in the
cast very much longer. Do you want to hear it?" Without
waiting for an answer she began to read: "My son has
told me everything you did for him. I would so like to
have you come to see us so that I can thank you in person. And Collin has a drawing for you he thinks you'd
like . . ."

"Don't look so surprised, Kathy. You always collect
grateful patients," Gail said affectionately.

"I'm a grateful patient, too," Matt said seriously.
"Without you and Steve, I never would have unraveled
my story."

"Hey! I thought this was going to be a party!" Steve, embarrassed at being thanked, avoided replying. He slipped a dance record on the machine, held out a hand and pulled Kathy up from her cushion. "Let's see if that ankle is as well as you claim."

The others arrived in a bunch, shortly afterwards— Jenny and Sean and Matt's photographer friend. To Gail's surprise, Keith Bowen, a young doctor from San Tomás, walked in with Linda and Jim.

"Miss Garfield caught me at the hospital just as she was going off duty," he explained. "She said I could come. We really miss you girls at San Tomás."

Everybody in the room translated "you girls" into "Miss Kelley Jones" without the slightest difficulty. The young doctor looked around in sudden disappointment.

"Jonesy is on duty," Kathy said, and paused mischievously before adding, "She'll be along in a minute."

Kelley came straight from the hospital. She was still in uniform. Her arms were filled with flowers.

"I never can resist that old man on the corner," she said, thrusting the bouquet at Gail.

"Something's happened to you," Linda said, looking at her shrewdly. "You look—different. Have they made you supervisor already? Come on—give."

With suppressed excitement, Kelley pulled an envelope from her pocket. Two airplane tickets fluttered to the floor.

"Our orders have come for Alaska! We leave in a week." She held out the official-looking documents to Kathy.

"Wonderful! Let's see!" came a chorus of voices.

But Kathy's voice was not among them. Unexpected tears came to her eyes, her heart flip-flopped, and her skin prickled. In sudden panic she fled to the kitchen.

When Steve followed her a moment later she was pouring coffee with a shaking hand, and tears were dripping into the cup.

"What's the matter?" he said. "Got the last-minute shivers?"

Kathy nodded dumbly. *Alaska is so far away from home—and you,* she was thinking.

"You shouldn't. It's a chance girls don't often get, to travel, to see other parts of the world. It might not come again."

"You *want* me to go!" she sobbed, hurt feelings suddenly replacing her panic. She knew that nursing in the Alaska hospital would be wonderful experience. She wanted to go—and yet she wanted to stay. But it was infuriating to have Steve accept so casually her absence for a whole year.

"You're getting your coffee all salty," said Steve. He took the cup out of her hands and set it on the table.

"I do want you to go," he went on, holding her hands firmly in his. "But I haven't told you the real reason. I thought there would be more time, and nothing is signed yet on the dotted line. Here's the story: I'm getting a year's leave from the Department, Kathy, for field study in forest conservation. *And* I'll have a month or so in Alaska."

"Steve!"

He kissed her lightly and let her go.

"Up there in the wilds," he said, "I might break a leg. It will be handy to have an R.N. around!"